DRAGON CAULDRON

Laurence Yep

DRAGON CAULDRON

R
003

HarperCollins*Publishers*

Library of Congress Cataloging in Publication Data
Yep, Laurence.
   Dragon cauldron / Laurence Yep.
      p.   cm.
   Summary: A dragon named Shimmer, a monkey wiz-
ard, a reformed witch, and two humans go on a quest to
mend the magic cauldron needed to repair the dragon's
home.
   ISBN 0-06-026753-4. — ISBN 0-06-026754-2 (lib. bdg.)
   [1. Dragons—Fiction.   2. Fantasy.]   I. Title.
PZ7.Y44Do   1991   90-39584
[Fic]—dc20   CIP
                                                        AC

Typography by Joyce Hopkins
1 2 3 4 5 6 7 8 9 10
First Edition

To Esteban,
who already knows
his own mind

DRAGON CAULDRON (also Baldy's bowl or the Bowl). For the earlier history of the cauldron see the entries under *Baldy* and *Serpent Lady*. . . . The most curious episode in the powerful vessel's history came in the 376th year of Sambar the Strong's rule. At that time the Princess Shimmer recognized her clan's greatest enemy, the Witch called Civet, who had stolen the waters of the inland Sea from her clan.

Rescued by a human boy, Thorn (see *Dragon Friend*), Shimmer became friends with him, eventually catching up with the Witch at the city of River Glen. However, Civet was able to loose the waters to destroy the city and escape with the help of the magical mist stone. This was due mainly to the negligence of the creature called Monkey (see *Great Pest*).

Seeking revenge, Shimmer and Thorn tracked Civet to her lair in the Weeping Mountain. Though she was able to overcome them at first, the clever Thorn was able to turn the tables on her, capture the Witch and save Shimmer.

Determined to restore the sea to its original site, Shimmer and Thorn gave the captured mist stone and Civet to the High King of the dragons. When he refused to help them, they stole the cauldron from the very middle of the High King's own treasure vault, aided by Monkey and a human girl named Indigo (see also under *Dragon Friend*) as well as the Witch Civet, who, though she had lost most of her powers with the mist stone, promised to do what she could to repair the damage that she had done. Unfortunately, in the escape the cauldron was itself cracked.

On Monkey's advice they returned to the mainland, there to seek the creatures known as the Smith and the Snail Woman, who, Monkey thought, could repair the broken cauldron. They had planned to drop Indigo off at her clan's village on the way, but found the famous forest in decay and her ancestral village on the verge of dying. Indigo then decided to continue on with Shimmer to help her in her quest. However, they had no sooner set out when war against all dragons was escalated by the then human king, the infamous Butcher. . . .

From *Meanderings in Dragon Antiquities* by the
Lady Francolin.

CHAPTER ONE

Moving quick and quiet . . .
Slipping among the shadows of the tall trees . . .
The Monkey Sage is loose within the woods. . . .
Tremble, you kings. Hide, you mighty dragons. . . .

"What was that, Monkey?" Thorn asked in a low voice.

It took me a moment to collect my thoughts from writing my little epic. "What was what?"

"It was a flash of blue." His eyes searched the forest around us.

I looked all around the trees but didn't see anything. People called it the Green Darkness, but they ought to have called it the Green Bore because it was green wherever you looked. Leafy vines and even shrubs grew on the trunks of the giant trees, so we were surrounded by monotonous green walls and even the light that managed to fall through the leaves high overhead was green and gloomy. And it was so hot and humid in the forest that I felt as if someone were dragging me through a tank of algae. Personally, give me a nice pine-covered mountain with plenty of waterfalls.

"I don't see anything," I said.

"It was right there." Thorn pointed.

Now Shimmer, being a dragon, was automatically sure that her eyes were better than a human's. "It was probably a bird, you fool ape," she insisted.

Thorn looked at Indigo's hair, which was still greased into blue spikes. "It looked like a human with a hairdo—a Kingfisher hairdo."

Indigo's robe had gotten snagged on a bush, and she stood there dumbfounded as if she didn't know what to do next. But then I reminded myself that she had been raised undersea in the dragon kingdoms, so even the experience of walking was something new and different. She gave a preoccupied mutter, "It was probably a bird. Maybe even a kingfisher."

And that was when Civet—of all people—stuck up for Thorn. "I saw it. And it wasn't a bird, because it didn't look like a bird."

Before she had lost almost all her powers as a Witch, she had done terrible things to Shimmer's people; and even now, despite all her oaths to help us regain their sea, none of us were too sure. "You've got very good eyes," Shimmer said skeptically.

A breeze blew through the trees and the leaves rustled. Civet's head lifted suddenly; and for a moment, just for a moment, the sullen look left her face. "I was born in a forest much like this one. A kingfisher would have been nearer the water."

Indigo tugged her robe free and there was a tearing sound. "So maybe one of my people is out hunting for berries."

Civet nodded her head at the thorny bush in amusement. "Judging from that bush, it's the wrong season for berries."

Indigo's momentum made her take a step backward, almost onto a large beetle that clicked its wing case in warning. She backed up in distaste until she bumped into Shimmer. "This is my forest, not yours."

In contrast to Indigo, Civet was gazing around her as if she were in paradise. "What do *you* know? You were raised in a dragon palace under the sea."

"But my parents told me about this place," Indigo

countered angrily. She always seemed to have a chip on her shoulder.

"Of course they did," Shimmer soothed her.

Poor Thorn. I could see that he was doing his best not to feel jealous, but Indigo had become a kind of pet to Shimmer ever since the dragon had rescued her from the dragon palace kitchens—from the salad dish, for all I knew.

Civet put up a hand. "Quiet."

We were silent for a moment, but the nervous girl couldn't stay still for long.

"I don't hear anything," Indigo finally said.

Civet smiled in a superior way. "That's just the point. A forest should be full of noise—birds, monkeys, bugs. Or didn't your parents tell you?"

As Indigo swelled herself up with some angry response, I cut in quickly. "Perhaps it was hunters," I suggested, "from Indigo's clan."

Civet scanned around her. "They're awful hunters then, because they're scaring away the game."

"My people are expert hunters," Indigo insisted.

Shimmer grunted. "Well, Civet's point is well taken. Someone unused to the woods is near. We should be more cautious. New disguises, everyone."

"I want to be a boy," Indigo said quickly.

"Done." Shimmer spread out her forepaws and

paused theatrically. If she hadn't been a dragon, I think she should have gone onto the stage. With a touch to the power of the pearl hidden in her forehead and a muttered spell and a sign, Shimmer changed Indigo into a boy in a ragged robe.

Civet became one of the Kingfisher clan, Indigo's folk. And the next moment so was Thorn.

"And now for this." Shimmer set her cauldron down. She never let it out of her sight if she could help it. It could boil away the waters of an entire ocean. With it she hoped to gather the sea that Civet had once stolen and restore it to her old home.

The next moment there was an old gourd there. Indigo and Thorn lunged for it at the same time, but Indigo snatched it up first. "I'll carry it," she said, giving Thorn a shove. Thorn looked as if he wanted to protest; but when Shimmer shook her head at him, Thorn held his tongue.

I had the good sense to disguise myself as an elderly man in an ordinary green robe. But when Shimmer had transformed herself, I nodded to her gown of green silk with designs in gold thread. "Why bother with disguises? That robe of yours announces to the whole world that you're a princess."

Ever since she had returned to the dragon kingdoms after a long exile, Shimmer had become harder to deal with. She tilted up her head so I could see her nose in profile—beak, really. (Her vanity would never let her have a human-size "snout.")

"I," she declared firmly, "cannot fall completely beneath my station."

"But there may be robbers in the woods," I suggested. "And then there are those who would envy someone like you."

Shimmer pointed at a muddy spot on her robe, and Indigo knelt quickly to rub vigorously at the offending spot.

But Thorn, who had been with her longest, knew how to handle the dragon. "True," he pretended to agree with her, "but as it stands now your old lady has no mystery." He quoted a line from an old song: "She has no air of sorrow."

Maybe someday you'll be traveling with a dragon; and if you do, keep in mind that you can get them to jump off a cliff—if you can just appeal to their sense of drama. "Yes-s-s," Shimmer agreed thoughtfully. Thorn had touched the ham within the dragon. "*She* would have something nobly tragic in her past."

Thorn was quick to pick up on that. "She would look as if she's seen better days."

"And we could be her menagerie," Civet said

sourly. She couldn't disguise her cynical, knowing smile.

But Shimmer ignored her as she became caught up in the role. "Just the thing, Thorn." And at a muttered spell her robe became more threadbare. "And, of course, all the rest of you should look a little worse for wear."

In the fork of a tree some old bark and leaves had rotted into a dirty lump. With a sigh, I picked up a handful and began to rub it on my robe. "Well, why waste magic?"

But then Indigo smiled slyly at Thorn. "No amount of dirt or ragged clothes can disguise his good looks. What he needs is a wart—right on his nose."

Shimmer finished examining her own personal artistry. "Yes, I think you may be right."

Even as Thorn opened his mouth to protest, a huge wart popped up at the tip of his nose. No matter where he looked, he could see the bump swaying in front of him. "It's going to make me cross-eyed."

Indigo was a sly one, she was. "So much the better for the disguise," she said, giggling.

As we began to move along the trail again, Shimmer hissed to me. "Don't move so fast, you idiot.

You're supposed to be an old man of sixty. You don't skip from root to root."

(Ha! What could a dragon tell Monkey about fooling people?) Placing a wrinkled hand on my chest, I announced, "I am a retired acrobat."

A dragon, any dragon, is trouble. And a princess is double that. Shimmer wrinkled her forehead and her nose started wriggling—an impressive sight for anyone. I dug in my paws—I mean feet—took a big lungful of air and got ready for a real row with this foolish dragon when Thorn spoke up again.

"Well," he said, looking disappointed, "if you can't make the full change . . ."

I could see the superior look on the dragon's face. As if I couldn't act rings around her! "Of course *I* can," I said. Slowly I bent forward and raised a leg and let it tremble as I lowered it. "I can be older than anyone." I winked at Thorn. "In fact, I probably am." And I began to shuffle along the trail.

Thorn slowed his pace to keep from getting ahead of me. "The real challenge is not being too young *or* too old."

I swung my head around slowly to gaze at him. "You know an awful lot about acting, don't you?"

"A lot of traveling theaters stopped at the inn I worked in," he explained hastily.

For a moment I wondered if he was playing the same game with me that he had played with Shimmer. "You aren't trying to fool old Monkey, are you?" I whispered to him.

"Oh, no," he said, and held out his arm to me. "I wouldn't dare."

"Humph. The world's full of critics." And I took his arm for support.

As we walked on through the great forest, Indigo still kept looking all around like a tourist. And I can't say that she looked very happy about what she was seeing.

She tripped for the dozenth time and sprawled in the thick layer of old leaves and dirt.

"Careful." Shimmer bent down. I thought it was to help Indigo, but she was checking on the gourd that was slung around Indigo's shoulders.

"Maybe I'd better carry that now." Thorn tried to take the gourd from her.

"It's still my turn." Indigo got up quickly, rubbing her ankle. "This stupid forest isn't what I really imagined it would be like," she said, and kicked at the offending vine.

Thorn scratched his head. "What did you think it would be like?"

Indigo began limping along like someone who had

been dumped into the middle of a garbage heap. "Not quite so messy."

Shimmer was quick to defend Indigo, the way she always was. I think she felt a little guilty for the way the child had been treated in the dragon kitchens. "You're just not used to walking on dry land yet," she said. "It took me nearly a century. All these nasty rocks and roots. It's so much nicer to swim."

"Or to fly," I said, looking up wistfully. But there wasn't a patch of sky to be seen—only a green ceiling of leaves.

And then the patrol stepped out onto the path about fifty meters ahead. "Halt," one of them shouted.

CHAPTER TWO

Five spearmen fanned across the narrow trail and into the trees on either side. And then an officer in glittering armor and a plumed helmet pointed a sword at us. "Let's see your passes."

I blinked my eyes innocently. "Passes?"

The officer regarded me as if I were crazy. "There's a war on with the dragons—or aren't you aware?"

"Yes, of course, officer." I searched my robe and then glanced at Shimmer. "Show them the passes, dear."

"I don't have any passes," Shimmer snapped.

I spread my hands. "I'm sorry. My wife must have left the passes back at home."

The officer turned. "Are these the suspicious ones?"

A man limped on his peg leg out from behind the

troops. I recognized him from Indigo's village the time we had tried to return her there. It was his indigo hair I had seen. Scratching his head between the blue spikes, he studied us a good long time. "I don't recognize the others, but no one can forget a nose that big." And he pointed straight at Shimmer.

The officer nodded to his men. "Let's take them back to the fort for questioning."

We might still have been able to talk our way out of trouble, but Indigo shouted, "Traitor, I'll cut out your tongue. How dare you turn us in. You're a disgrace to our clan."

As she started a furious charge forward, the peg-legged man stumbled back behind the soldiers. "You little fool. The clan is no more! It's broken up, dispersed."

Thorn caught Indigo around the waist and lifted her kicking into the air. "Revenge can wait," he panted.

We still might have been able to get away if the others had left the talking to me; but for such long-lived creatures, dragons can be exasperatingly impatient.

"This disguise was getting itchy anyway," Shimmer said, and, touching her forehead, she started to change herself back into her true form.

Of course, while Shimmer was busy transforming herself, she was a very convenient target. Left to herself, she would have been chopped into little green bits. So I didn't bother to change my own self back into my real form.

Instead, I just reached behind my ear and took out what looked like a needle. "Change!" I yelled, and the next moment I was twirling an iron rod in my hand with a gold loop at either end. I brandished it over my head affectionately, listened to the lovely swishing sound it made whirling through the air.

And Shimmer raised a hand that was already green and whose fingers had lengthened into claws. "I think you ought to run along now," she said to the officer.

"I don't think so," the officer said, and gestured toward the bushes. Immediately another five soldiers emerged, each with a cocked crossbow. At a nod from the officer, one of them raised his weapon to his shoulder and pushed a button. The string twanged and the bolt thunked several centimeters into a nearby tree.

I stared at the bolt thoughtfully. "That could go through even a dragon's hide."

"Or," Shimmer grumbled, "even through something as thick as a monkey's skull."

"Her people aren't at war with you," Indigo tried to explain. "It's the other dragons you want." She meant the war that the king of the humans, the Butcher, had declared against another clan of dragons—though how he was going to conquer them was anybody's guess.

But the officer didn't seem interested in technicalities. "Surrender or die!"

"That's a coward's weapon," I taunted them.

A second bolt pinned my cap to a tree trunk. Thorn yanked it free and held it out to me. "I don't think insults are going to scare them away."

I pulled the cap back over the gold circlet around my head. "I think," I muttered to Shimmer, "that we'd better fly strategically to the rear. I can take care of these bundles. Can you take the other two?"

"What?" Indigo whispered.

"He means fly out of here," Thorn said in a low voice.

Shimmer leaned her head toward me. "There's not enough room for me to spread my wings. And anyway, the tree branches above us are like a maze. While we tried to find our way through, these soldiers would be turning us into porcupines."

But Shimmer wasn't the only proud one. "I won't be treated like a piece of garbage." Civet strode past me before I could stop her. Throwing up her hands, she commanded, "Halt! I am a powerful Witch. Anger me at your peril."

Though Shimmer had changed Civet back into her true shape as well, she was less than impressive. Her robes were as ragged as a beggar's. Though she wore a royal ransom in jewelry, the gems were so large and ostentatious that the soldiers probably assumed they were fake. At any rate, after gazing at the spectacle for a moment, they began to laugh.

"You have decided your own fate." Civet made abrupt passes with her hands and stabbed a finger at a tree. "Bind them."

When the tree stayed as it was, the soldiers began to laugh even harder. I used a loop of my staff to hook her arm. "I tip my cap to you. It's not everyone who tries to kill an enemy with laughter."

A crestfallen Civet let herself be tugged back. "*All* my magic's gone," she said in surprise as she stumbled backward.

In the meantime the officer had drawn his sword and swung it toward a pair of soldiers. Putting down their spears, they took out chains and manacles and began to advance.

"Can't you shrink us?" Indigo asked out of the side of her mouth to Shimmer.

"Now why didn't I think of that?" I tugged my now holey cap tighter on my head.

"It's too simple," Indigo snapped.

Shimmer watched the soldiers moving forward warily. "I'll need time."

"You've got it." With a spring, I leaped into the air and began to somersault rapidly as if on an invisible floor.

The soldiers in front of me cringed, but I whipped right over them. They had the look of garrison troops who were used to catching poachers when they weren't tending their own vegetable patches. The patrol hadn't spread out so that they would have new lines of fire. Instead, they had stayed where they were, and the pair with the chains blocked the fire of most of the patrol. It was only a soldier on either extreme end who could still shoot.

I landed before the startled officer and then sprang to the end of the line. Looping my staff over the head of that soldier, I gave a yank that sent him into another pair.

Then I pivoted for a spring at the man at the other end, but I saw him aiming at someone.

"Dragons, dragons, dragons," I heard Thorn shouting. The boy had realized what I was up to and had charged the other side. Well, Shimmer had always said that the boy had more courage than sense.

"Catch," I said. And with a flick of my wrist I sent the staff twirling toward the crossbowman. It whirled so fast that it spun in a kind of circle.

The soldier had time to look up, startled, and then the staff had knocked him to the ground. The unfortunate part about that maneuver was that it left me unarmed.

I heard a hissing sound like a little viper and ducked just in time as the officer's sword blade sliced through the air right where my head had been.

Squatting, I reached up with one hand and caught his belt by the buckle. My other hand caught his ankle. I had intended to throw him through the air; but his buckle was weaker than it looked. It gave way the moment I seized it.

One moment he was standing there with his sword raised over his shoulder for a deadly backstroke and looking as fierce as a landlord. And the next moment his pants had bagged down around his boot tops, with his underwear on display for all the world. Behind him one of his men snickered.

As he looked down in surprise, I butted his belly

with my head. And though my head wasn't as hard as a dragon's, the air whooshed out of him and he fell backward on top of two of his men.

With a little apologetic shrug I jumped into the air. A couple of bounces and I was standing on top of the fallen soldier's head. "I think this is mine." And then I had my staff back in my hands.

By then the first two soldiers had dropped their chains and had grabbed Thorn. "We got one. We got one," the soldiers were shouting. But I think there was room for argument, because one soldier lay sprawled in the dirt while Thorn sat on his head. And the other soldier had his helmet twisted halfway while he tried to hold the wriggling Thorn.

"Get away, get away," a tiny voice shouted from above. Shimmer, now the size of a bird, was circling up toward the forest canopy; and Civet and Indigo were so small that I could not see either of them.

I shoved my staff into the belly of the upright soldier, and he doubled up with a grunt. And then a tap with the other end of my staff put the second soldier to sleep. Catching Thorn by the collar, I lifted him into the air and plopped him down beyond the clearing.

We dashed off the trail straight through a bush

[*18*]

with nasty, needlelike spines and into trees themselves. A bolt thunked into another tree.

"Hurry, hurry," Shimmer called from far overhead.

"Change," I shouted, and my staff shrank to the size of a needle so I could tuck it behind my ear. And then I squatted down. "Hop on, boy."

The next moment Thorn had climbed on my back. With his arms wrapped around my neck and his legs around my waist, I began to somersault through the air. "By the way, you don't get airsick, do you?"

"Not on Shimmer," he said shakily.

"That's like riding on an old barge when you could be on a racing yacht. Now we'll really see," I warned. A bolt slammed several meters beneath us into a tree trunk. I could have gotten into the forest canopy faster if I could have climbed straight, but I was busy dodging those pesky bolts.

The real problem was that these giant trees were all smooth trunk for some fifty meters before their branches began. And in the meantime the forest floor below was crawling with crossbowmen who wanted to play shoot-the-monkey.

But suddenly a large stick whizzed past. And then

there was a second. I sprang to a tree on my left and dug my fingers into the slippery bark. "What's going on?"

From the tree up above there was a regular rain of sticks along with clumps of moss and flower-covered vines. Far below, there was a loud metallic bong as if a branch had bounced off a helmet. When I glanced down, I saw the crossbowmen ducking.

"Hurry up," Shimmer called down to us. I could just make out her shadowy shape within the forest canopy—like a fish glimpsed in a murky pond. She had changed herself back to her usual size and was jumping up and down in the top of one tree.

Above us the tree branches and moss shook and swayed until it looked as if the tree itself were dancing. Sheets of moss and even branches crashed down.

"Time to put your friend on a diet." I winked at Thorn. And then, with a bound, I was leaping into the air, somersaulting upward as if there were invisible steps.

CHAPTER THREE

Grinning, I leaped into the air and climbed toward the glittering green roof above.

In a forest as old as the Green Darkness, the trees grow so tall that their tops are a hundred meters above the ground and the leafy branches grow together in a dense tangle. Vines grow around the branches, weaving them into an even denser tangle. Leaves fall, gathering and decaying in the hollows of branches, so bushes and small trees can grow even there, their strange roots crawling around the host tree like strange, frozen snakes.

If the forest floor seems a monotonous green, the forest top bursts with colors. All sorts of orchids and other exotic flowers bloom among the treetops, splashing color everywhere. Birds, bright as rainbows, streak among the trees, and even my ape cousins have bright fur and stripes.

I made my way up a few branches and then sat down to get my wind back. "I think," I panted, "that we're out of range now. Everybody off." I tapped at Thorn's wrists, so he let go of my neck and climbed down beside me.

A fuzzy white head peered out at us from a pink, cup-shaped flower. "Don't touch that thing," I warned Thorn. "It's poisonous."

With a screech the creature hopped into the air and spread its legs so that the flaps of flesh could spread out like a kite, and it glided away.

"Well, I don't think this disguise will work anymore." With a wrinkle of my nose and a shake of my shoulders, I changed myself into my true monkey shape and than I inspected my robe—the real one. The yellow cloth was stained, but nothing that a good scrubbing couldn't take out. The tiger skin was fine.

"Now me," Thorn said impatiently.

"Sorry, but you have to wait for the person who changed you; and that's Shimmer."

As we sat upon the branch, we could hear the forest canopy shaking. More branches and moss fell as Shimmer made her way over to us.

"Over here, you overgrown piece of luggage," I called.

Shimmer's head snaked out of a mass of greenery. "Bother passengers anyway," she grumbled. She sprang into the air and landed overhead on our tree, sinking her claws into the thick tree trunk like a cat. The next moment she was slithering down to us as nimbly as a lizard. On her back a normal-sized Indigo and Civet clung desperately and looked green enough to match the forest top.

"Better make room for the barge." I nudged Thorn to move farther along the branch. It dipped alarmingly when Shimmer crawled out onto it.

"You couldn't have shrunk back to a smaller size?" I frowned as the branch swayed like a boat in a storm.

"I have to be a proper length," Shimmer explained coolly. "And anyway, all that shrinking and expanding gives me a headache."

I was going to say something about how her pea-sized brain ought to fit in any size skull; but Indigo slid off Shimmer's back and huddled in a heap against her side. At first I thought she was sick, but then she wailed, "This isn't home."

Civet climbed down beside her. "This is the Green Darkness," she reminded her.

Indigo raised her blue-spiked head. "But it's not like I thought at all. I don't fit in here. I don't fit in anywhere." Like Thorn, she had already done so much during our adventures that it was easy to forget that she was a child—until she wept. She had been an orphan, alone in the High King's palace. Shimmer, seeing a bit of her own crusty self in the human girl, had tried to take her back to her people's village; but we had found her home in decay and her people dispersed.

Civet looked down with thinly veiled contempt and Shimmer looked around uncomfortably. Finally, she lifted a paw with claws that could have sliced through armor and patted Indigo awkwardly on the back. "Nonsense. We'd be dead now if it weren't for you."

Indigo lifted her face. The tears had made stripes in the dirt on her cheeks. "Really?"

"Of course," Shimmer assured her. "A clever girl like you can fit in anywhere. Didn't you just save our lives?"

Indigo nodded toward us. "Thorn and Monkey were the brave ones."

"What's bravery if you can't find your way out of a trap?" Shimmer waved a paw vaguely in the air. "It was your idea for me to shrink so I could fly us out of there."

"But," Indigo said uncertainly, "Thorn was the one who spotted the trap in the first place."

"Bah! You would have seen it soon enough." Indigo was sitting with her back to Shimmer, so she couldn't see the dragon's forepaw gesturing toward Thorn. "Isn't that right, Thorn?"

The wart trembled indignantly on the tip of Thorn's nose. It's hard enough to be brave; but it's twice as hard to give the glory to someone else. But Thorn was a big enough person for that. "That's right."

I might have spoken up for Thorn—and myself as well. But suddenly there wasn't time for sorting out all the hurts and pleasantries. A crossbow twanged, and a bolt buried itself into the trunk of our tree. I whirled around. In the tree next to us, a crossbowman was busy rewinding his crossbow. At the same time, another crossbowman was rising through the air on an invisible platform.

"A wizard must have joined them," I said, and squatted. "Hop on, boy."

As soon as I felt his hands around my neck, I was leaping through the air. Another bolt crashed through the branches. Below us, a third crossbowman rose to join the others.

[25]

Shimmer shifted and stamped, but every time she tried to unfold her wings, she bumped into branches or some other obstruction. "I can't spread my wings," she moaned.

"Climb up to the top of the trees," I shouted to her.

In the forest canopy even someone as big as Shimmer would be hidden quickly. What worried me was what other magic the wizard might have in store.

About thirty meters on, the tree trunk began to narrow. I scampered up the rest of the trunk eagerly until I emerged into the sunlight and blue sky. "Ha! I'd like to see them catch me now."

"Coming through," Shimmer shouted from below. Branches snapped and crashed below as she clawed her way up the tree trunk. There was only one way to escape, and that was up.

With a leap, I sprang into the air. "This should be good," I whispered to Thorn.

As the heavy dragon climbed up the tree, its top began to whip back and forth. And as she poked her snout out of the tree canopy, the tree itself began to bend backward.

"Jump!" I shouted down to her.

"Jump?" she said indignantly. "I'll have you know that I'm famous for the grace of my takeoffs."

From our left, brightly feathered birds squawked and flew up in flocks—as if a rainbow were disintegrating around us. The wizard was up to something. "Your head will be gracing some mantlepiece if you don't take off. Or," I added with a michievous laugh, "do you need a push?"

I think it was my teasing that finally made up Shimmer's mind. The trees shook underneath her and we heard a thunderous crack. The treetop had broken off when she had pushed away. Her head poked up above the trees, and then the rest of her came scrambling and twisting over the tops of the trees.

The thin upper branches seemed to break the moment her paws touched them, but she managed to spread her wings. Then, in one great flap, she rose into the air.

The spectacle was so hilarious that I couldn't help slapping my thighs and laughing. "So much for the grace of dragons."

"Shh, she might hear you," Thorn tried to hush me. He was still loyal to her despite everything.

With another flap of her wings she soared past us. "Too late. I already did." But she was grinning. "It's good to be flying again!" While Indigo and Civet clung to her desperately, Shimmer coiled and looped her long, sinuous body through the air. "None of this skulking along like frogs in the dirt. Maybe I've spent so much time on the ground that I'd begun to think like a groundhog instead of like a flier."

She banked suddenly and roared by us, tumbling us in the winds left by her passage. "Let's see you keep up with me now, you stupid Monkey."

"You're in for it now," Thorn said.

"Think so?" I asked. Shimmer was already a dot in the sky. Laughing, I set off after her.

We caught up with them after two kilometers— I suppose when Shimmer had judged that she had punished us enough. We flew on over the Green Darkness. The forest tops rolled on like the frozen waves of a green sea. Here and there a flock of birds flew up in the air and wheeled about in a small cloud of dots. And every now and then some lonely ape would screech up at us. But there was no sign of pursuit. We were free to go on to the Smith's mountain.

When the sky began to redden with sunset, we reached the edge of the forest itself. Ahead of us rolled the barrens in broad stretches of scrub and weeds.

As we flew over the forest, I gave a shiver. At

least the Green Darkness, for all of its monotony, was alive. Ahead of us was nothing but a long, lifeless stretch. "I'll be glad when we're beyond the barrens."

From the back, Thorn tried to sound confident. "Shimmer and I have gone through worse. You should have seen the salt desert."

"This was once the Fragrant Kingdom, famous for all the different types of flowers that grew here," I said. "But the Nameless One destroyed it."

I could feel Thorn shift as he tried to get a better look at what was below. "Who's the Nameless One?"

I clicked my tongue. "It isn't good that you humans are forgetting him. He was once a king with a powerful army and even more powerful magic; for they say he was indestructible. He joined with evil creatures like the Keeper. So the Five Masters—the Unicorn, the Archer, the Serpent Lady, the Lord of the Flowers and Calambac the Dragon—fought them, and all good creatures joined with them. But when the evil ones were defeated, the Five Masters found they couldn't kill the Nameless One. So they stripped him of his powers and even his name and punished him in a terrible way."

But trying to answer Thorn's questions was like

opening up a puzzle box in which there is an even smaller one and so on and on. "What sort of punishment?" he wanted to know.

"My master wouldn't tell me except to say that I should hope it never happens to me." I pointed below. In the lengthening shadows we could make out the traces of broad roads and even the outlines of buildings. "The war destroyed everything; and what it didn't destroy, the winds and the rains have razed."

"It's not like you to give up so easily on getting an answer," Thorn said.

I fingered the yellow robe underneath my tiger skin. "When you're the disciple of a mighty wizard, you have to know when to satisfy your thirst for knowledge and when to be discreet." It was perhaps stretching the truth a bit; but I've always felt the truth was something that should be "improved" every now and then. Truth to tell, there had been something in my master's voice and face that had scared the curiosity right out of me.

Occasionally a ruined tower rose from the land like a crumbling fang. And slowly the land itself began to rise in rows of hills. We covered another ten kilometers before the sun finally disappeared behind the mountains.

"We'd better make camp," I suggested. Below us was the bronze oval of a lake. And suddenly I had an idea about how to pay Shimmer for the insults back in the forest.

Shimmer nodded her agreement. "I think we've escaped our pursuers."

"Are you as bad on landings as you are on take-offs?" I barely dodged out of the way of a vicious swipe of her tail.

"Hey, remember who's an innocent passenger," Thorn yelped.

But Shimmer was too angry to apologize. "I can't help it if I have to be large enough to carry two people."

"There's a lake below." I pointed down at it. "Race you."

"Whoa," Thorn tried to shout, but I had already stopped dead.

"This is where it pays not to be a big, old, fat dragon," I taunted. And the next moment we were dropping like a stone and I was waving my paw casually up at her. I glanced over my shoulder to see how Thorn was taking it. But his mouth was a big, frightened hole in his face.

The next moment Shimmer shot past us. Even in her best moods she didn't like to be teased. But she was especially sensitive about her flying. I had to cartwheel through the air to regain my balance.

"Stupid, slow fur bag." Her voice drifted upward to us.

"This should be good," I chuckled as I righted myself and began to follow her.

Now I like Thorn, but he is too earnest for his own good. He wouldn't know a good joke if he tripped over it. "You shouldn't play tricks on her like this," he said.

"Well, I do admit it's shamelessly easy," I agreed. Arching my hands over my head, I dove after her. "But the pompous old windbag had it coming."

The bronze oval swelled into the size of a kidney bean and then even larger. We could see the last rays of the sunlight winking in red lines over the surface.

"Time to stop." I tucked my knees in against my chest so that I tumbled head over heels. Suddenly I kicked out my legs, and we stopped as if we had landed on some invisible ledge. I looked over my shoulder at Thorn and winked. "I wonder if Shimmer thinks cleverness is still more important than bravery, eh? Should we ask her?"

The boy squirmed uncomfortably, as if he didn't

enjoy being part of my trick. I sighed. "It's more important than speed, at any rate."

Shimmer, however, had misjudged her dive, as I had known she would. I could see her arching her back and spreading her wings as she tried to pull out. But it was too late.

"Oh, no-o-o-o!" Her angry wail drifted slowly up toward us. "I guess you win," I called down cheerfully.

"You dratted ape!" Her paws made white henscratches on the surface of the lake. And the next moment she and her passengers were plowing right into the water.

Laughing, I tumbled onto the shore of the lake. "We'd better get some wood and get a fire going, boy."

Thorn lowered his legs from around my waist and stamped them as if he were grateful finally to touch the ground. "Aren't you going to make fun of Shimmer?"

I could hear her spluttering in the lake and winked at the boy. "How do you think I've survived so long despite all the pranks I've played? I know when to stop."

And I began to pick up fuel diligently.

CHAPTER FOUR

By the time Shimmer and the others had pulled themselves out of the pond, I had some weeds and twigs burning. "We'll have you warm in a jiffy." I cheerfully waved a stick for them to sit down and then fed it to the fire.

Indigo and Civet sat down soggily, and Shimmer was too cold to chase me around. But she did shoot a few angry looks in my direction as she hunkered down. And I was smart enough always to keep the fire between myself and her. Since she was a dragon, her little plunge had wounded only her dignity— but then a dragon would rather lose a paw than a bit of pride.

Besides, Indigo did enough grumbling for the three of them. She looked around as if she loathed the whole idea of living on the land. "I didn't think anything could make that trashy forest seem better, but this place makes it look like paradise. Even the weeds around here give me the creeps."

The ground bordering the lake was covered with weeds like snakes coiling in and out among one another with nasty little thorns growing from the sides. The leaves were thin little slivers that drooped away like centipede legs. And there were tiny red flowers that looked like drops of blood.

"It's needleweed." Civet barely gave it a glance. "There's an old story that it once was the hair of a sorceress."

"How charming," Indigo mumbled, and tried to shift over to a clearer spot.

Shimmer had shrunk herself to two meters and crouched there like a giant cat. "So much for sneaking unannounced through the countryside. We might as well fly straight to the Smith." The Smith was an ancient creature who with his wife, the Snail Woman, produced all sorts of magical things from their forge.

I grunted my agreement as I got dinner ready. "From what we've seen, the Butcher must have been preparing for this war a long time."

Thorn squatted, feeding the fire. "I wonder how the dragons are doing."

Shimmer shrugged one shoulder. "The dragons

will sink every boat that tries to sail on the seas; and as long as they stay in the water, the humans can't reach them."

I watched the flames crackle up. "It's not like the Butcher to get into a war that he can't win. He's up to something."

"Whatever." Shimmer didn't really seem very worried about the threat of the Butcher. "It's speed that counts now. How many days to these friends of yours who can fix the cauldron?"

I scratched a claw in the dirt. "Two days' flight over the barrens to the mountains. That's the risky part, but it can't be helped. And then two more days through the mountains."

Shimmer curled up like a cat, steam rising from her scales. "Not much chance of our being seen. There shouldn't be a soul for kilometers. And the Butcher would have all his troops and spies on the coast."

I looked in the direction of the mountains, but it was too dark and they were still too far away to be seen even if it had been daytime. "From there," I said, absently, "we'll have to hope that the Snail Woman and the Smith see our signal."

Almost immediately I realized my mistake when Shimmer's head shot up. "You told us you could get the cauldron fixed; but you don't even know where to go?"

As a precaution, I slid over so that Thorn was also between me and Shimmer. "I do. Their smithy is on a mountain that appears when the sun rises at midnight."

Indigo narrowed her eyes. "There's no such thing."

Shimmer reared up, lashing her tail. "You idiot! You windbag! You don't know either the Smith *or* the Snail Woman, do you? And you certainly can't ask them for a favor."

If people would listen carefully, they wouldn't misunderstand me. "They know my master."

"Maybe we should go back to help Shimmer's people." Thorn used a large twig to poke at the fire.

"Never," Indigo said. She had no reason to love the dragons.

"Then why don't you stay?" Thorn snapped.

Indigo glared at him. "Because Shimmer saved me; and she tried to give me back my home." She shrugged off the recent painful memory. "She couldn't help it if it wasn't what I expected. I'll see that she gets a home, at least."

Shimmer hesitated and then settled down. "I can't do much until we restore the sea. Since we've come this far, we might as well see if they'll help us. If the Smith refuses"—she gave an ugly look at me— "then we'll go back to the dragon kingdoms. And you"—she nodded to Civet and then at Indigo— "and you will be released from your vows to help me restore the sea. The world is wide. I'm sure you'll find something in it that will compensate you for your losses."

"In the meantime," Thorn said, pointing to the wart on his nose, "I wouldn't mind being my true form."

Indigo lounged back, taking off the cauldron that was still disguised as a gourd. "Oh, I don't know. I think it makes you look more distinguished."

I'm afraid that Shimmer may have lumped him in with my prank, because she was quick to agree. "Yes. It lends you a certain air of grandeur."

Poor Thorn couldn't see that they were simply teasing. I'd heard he'd had a pretty hard life of it as a servant in a wretched little village inn. And the many beatings might have instilled discipline but not a sense of humor. I'm afraid that he took it rather as if Shimmer and Indigo were ganging up on him.

"Well," he said with as much dignity as he could, "when the grandeur begins to fade, you can change me back." He picked up one of the pots that Shimmer had made from a rock and tried to shove it at Indigo. "It's your turn to get water."

But Indigo shoved it away. "I did it last time."

He waved it at her. "No, you didn't."

Civet rose and held out her hand. Water dripped from her tattered robes as she looked around scornfully. "I'm sorry to see that the human race hasn't gotten any better. *I'll* get the water."

As Civet walked down toward the lake, Shimmer touched her forehead and muttered a spell and made a sign; and once again Thorn was back to his true shape. By now even a thickheaded dragon could tell that she had pushed Thorn too far. But do you think she apologized? No, that's too simple for a dragon.

Instead, she gave a little groan. "Thorn, dear," she said, "I'm so sore from flying. Will you give me a massage?"

Thorn was never the type to hold a grudge, even a mistaken one. He climbed up the dragon's tail onto her back and began to kick and stomp the tough hide between her wings.

Shimmer lay with her head on the ground and spread out her forepaws in sheer bliss. "Yes. Right there." Though Thorn was jumping up and down with solid thumps, she felt it only as gentle massage through her armorlike skin.

Sullenly Indigo squirmed around so her back was to Shimmer and Thorn. Well, I'm a great believer in keeping everyone happy, so I plopped down beside her. "It must have been hard for the only human in the dragon palace."

She sorted through some of the firewood we had gathered. "They were all pretty dumb, dragons and nondragons."

Her personality was as spiky as her hair, apparently. "There must have been some other servants in the same boat as you."

"They were either dumb or useless." She selected one large stick that we had taken from a bush and seemed to be weighing it in her hand.

I couldn't help feeling a little surprised. "A bright child like you must have had friends."

She shrugged, and the shrug told me all I wanted to know. It was as if she were throwing off any extra burdens. "I didn't need them."

"Then why go on with Shimmer?" I wondered.

"Shimmer is . . . different." She glanced over her shoulder at Shimmer, but the sight of her with Thorn made Indigo scowl. She's jealous, I said to myself. And then I realized that Shimmer was probably the one and only friend Indigo had ever had in her short life.

"Well, Monkey's your friend now." I tried to put my arm around her shoulder to give her a hug and got an elbow for my trouble—a very sharp, bony elbow, I might add.

"You're as dumb as the rest of them." And she threw the stick on the fire. The next moment there was a loud pop.

"What was that?" Shimmer reared up, startled, sending Thorn flying off her back into the grass.

The stick began to snap as the sap oozed out. "Thorn," Indigo said without turning around, "must have put on a stick of wood that was too green."

And she sat there with a very pleased expression, staring at the sap sizzling out of the wood. And I started to think that she might have deserved some of the beatings she said she'd had back in the dragon palace. As Shimmer helped Thorn up, I leaned over. "That was a sly prank," I said in a low voice.

She cradled her chin on top of her clasped hands. "You should know," she whispered back.

I sighed. Humans, in their own way, could be trickier than dragons. Give me a monster anytime— one who's set on gobbling you down for lunch. Then the relationship is straightforward and honest. You either knock the monster out or it tosses you down its throat. Simple, easy, no complications to deal with.

Dinner was some nuts we had gotten from Indigo's people and some salted fish that we had "borrowed" from the storerooms of the dragon palaces. But water would have helped immeasurably, so I looked for Civet.

Twisting around, I saw her kneeling beside the lake with the pot still in her lap.

"How about that water?" I called to her.

Civet, though, acted as if she didn't hear.

Humans, I decided, were worse than a dozen monsters. I started to walk down toward the lakeshore. "Are you all right?"

Civet was staring in fascination at the placid lake. It was almost a perfect oval about two hundred meters wide by a hundred. And the banks had sharp edges, as if the lake had been cut out with chisels. Though no wind marred the surface, a cold breeze seemed to rise from it, and I gave a shiver.

"What's wrong?" I shook Civet's shoulder.

She gazed at the water. "Can't you see it?"

Ever curious, Indigo had joined us by the lake, wrapping her arms around herself against the sudden chill. "All I see is my own reflection."

And looking at the lake, I could see a mirror-perfect image of the sky and our own faces. "There's a door right there." Civet pointed into the middle of the lake. "Right at the bottom."

"Of course," Indigo said, and tapped a finger against the side of her head.

But Civet could see Indigo's reflection. "It's there, I tell you."

By that time Shimmer and Thorn had come down as well to see what all the commotion was about. "What's there?" Shimmer wondered.

"A door." Thorn bent over curiously. "It's all of some black stone."

"Obsidian," Civet identified it. "People once used it for knives and axe heads."

Shimmer and I exchanged glances. Perhaps it hadn't been such a good idea to camp by the lake. "All that splashing around in the lake may have woken up something," I suggested.

Shimmer raised a paw and took Civet's arm. "Then it would be wise to go back to the fire."

I backed away so I could keep my eyes on the lake. "And it might be smart to keep watch tonight."

Indigo looked at us as if we were all crazy. "I thought this land belonged to the enemies of the Nameless One?"

"They were his enemies because they were rivals

for power, not because they were especially vir-
tuous. The Five Masters took their allies where they
could find them; but they were not always comfortable with them." Shimmer tried to lift Civet to
her feet.

But she tried to fight off the dragon. "There's
magic down there. I can feel it." She looked at the
lake hungrily—as if she were a starving dog and it
were a bone.

"Then it's magic that should be left alone." Gently
but firmly, Shimmer drew Civet to her feet. "In
those early days before the Great War, people were
not always scrupulous about how spells were
worked."

I nodded, remembering my master's stories. "The
magicians hereabouts took paths that we avoid now-
adays."

Indigo looked over at me curiously. "What sort
of paths?"

I plucked at her sleeve to keep her moving away
from the lakeshore. "For one thing, they would take
over another person's body."

Indigo wrinkled her nose. "How'd they do that?"

"They'd send their soul into another body," I explained.

Thorn got the idea sooner than Indigo. "Like pouring new wine into an old skin."

"Yes, except that the old wine sometimes didn't have any place to go." I had to give a chuckle. "There's the tale of a magician who switched around so many times that he forgot what his original body looked like. He wound up being stuck inside a snake and having to stay that way because his sort of magic needed two hands to work the spells."

"It wasn't honor that made them turn away from those arts." Civet held the pot between her hands. "It was as dangerous for the practitioner as for the victim."

Shimmer studied her closely. "Just how much do you know about it?"

"I heard tales. That's all." Blinking her eyes, she glanced at me and then glanced away again.

"What about the water?" Thorn pointed to the pot that Civet was still clasping.

Shimmer kept her eyes on the surface, but the lake was calm. "I think it would be wiser to go thirsty tonight than to disturb the lake any further."

CHAPTER FIVE

I thought Indigo would tease our two "mystics" during dinner, but she was silent, every now and then her eyes glancing up at the darkening sky. Civet had us all pretty jumpy, but I couldn't help asking, "What's wrong?"

Indigo was trying her best not to gape. "Are those little bits of light stars?"

Shimmer chewed at a piece of fish. "Certainly. You never went to the surface at night?"

Indigo shook her head. "I was never on the surface period." Despite herself, she couldn't keep the awe from her voice. "My father tried to describe them. But he didn't tell me they would look so far away."

Shimmer spat out a bone. "All our troubles probably seem so small to the stars."

Indigo glanced at the dragon. "You must think I'm pretty dumb."

"No," Shimmer hastened to say. "It's like seeing the world with new eyes. In fact, you and I can keep the first watch together and I can show you all the constellations."

"If you want," Indigo said with a shrug. She was still so sensitive about being hurt that she was afraid even to show gratitude.

"Well, I'm turning in." Thorn turned as if he wanted to keep his back to the fire, but it also put Shimmer and Indigo out of his vision.

"Very well," Shimmer agreed. "Then Civet can take the next watch, and then you, and finally Monkey."

"That suits me." I got up and began to stomp my feet up and down. "We should sleep together for warmth just like sheep. But first we need to trample down the needleweed."

"You don't need to do your native dance. Just step back." And without waiting to see if I was clear, Shimmer started to roll back and forth. In her armored hide, she didn't feel a thing.

I jumped back barely in time. "I knew there was some use for traveling with an inflated toad like you."

Shimmer paused and eyed me. "Why don't you come a little closer, and I'll show you how much is hot air and how much is muscle."

"I already know how much is hot air," I snapped, but I took the precaution of stepping back out of range of her tail. And Shimmer was feeling too tired to argue. With a contemptuous snort she hunkered back down beside Indigo.

She really wasn't so bad for a dragon; and there are some who could misunderstand and say it was my fault that her people still didn't have a home. I had tried to get a little too fancy arresting Civet, and Civet had been able to loose the waters she had stolen from Shimmer's clan.

I lay down on Shimmer's lee side. Even so, a cold draft managed to find me. And despite all her rolling, it was still like lying on a bed of nails.

I lay down more for show than because I was sleepy. It wasn't Shimmer's astronomical lesson that kept me awake. A monkey's curiosity bump is always his or her greatest weakness; and I kept wondering who or what was at the bottom of the lake.

And when her watch was over, it was a wonder any of us could sleep. Lying next to a sleeping dragon may sound exciting; but it won't be until they invent a dragon that doesn't snore. It's like trying to sleep next to a mill wheel that's thumping and grinding along. And it's no fun if the dragon twitches her legs in her sleep.

And yet I must have been more weary than I thought, because I fell asleep somewhere around the dozenth time I thought about Civet's vision. And then I felt someone stir beside me. Waking instantly, I thought I could hear someone weeping softly.

Rolling over onto my other side, I could see Civet a few meters away. She had tied her hair loosely behind her. She sat with her arms wrapped around herself—and in the moonlight with her back turned, she seemed like the girl she must have been before her family had sacrificed her to a cruel spirit, the King Within the River, who had forced her to marry him.

The kindly Thorn had also heard the sound and had sat up. "Are you all right?" he asked softly.

When Civet turned, I couldn't see any sign of tears on her face. "Do you hear the crying too?"

Thorn crawled over toward her. "Yes. How long has it been going on?"

"Just a little while. I think it's coming from over there." And she looked toward the lake. "I'm going to go check."

Thorn looked back at the slumbering Shimmer, and I barely closed my eyes in time. "But she wanted us to stay away from the lake."

"No one's asking you to come," Civet whispered. I could hear her brushing off her robes.

Thorn hesitated, and I knew he was thinking of Indigo and how she had mocked them. The next moment I heard him get up as well.

Now if I had stopped them then, things might have turned out far better for Civet. But as my master says, they also might have turned out far worse. And as I said, a monkey's worst flaw is his or her curiosity bump. And mine was positively itching at that point.

So I got quietly to my feet and followed the other two. They were almost creeping across the needleweed. As a result, it was easy to catch up with them.

"Don't try to make me go back," Civet warned angrily.

I don't know what she could have done if I had picked her up and packed her back on my shoulder, but I tactfully did not say anything. "I'm just a little thirsty myself from all that salted fish, so I thought I'd take a little stroll down to the lake," I said, grinning.

Civet brightened for the first time that I had ever seen when she was talking to someone. "What a coincidence. So are we."

The weeping sounds grew louder as we approached the lakeshore; and when we were standing right at the edge of the water, Civet clutched at my arm and whispered in my ear. "It's coming from behind the door."

"Let's go back." I tried to draw her and Thorn away.

But at that moment a soft, silvery, rectangular outline shone from within the inky waters. And so help me, the needleweed began to move, writhing as if it were alive. Before I knew it, it was wrapped around my ankles. I tried to jump into the air, but it held me as unbreakably as chains. I glanced at Thorn and Civet, but they were both struggling to lift their legs and having no more luck than I was.

I was just about to shout for help when the needleweed suddenly lifted my right foot. That was so unexpected that I looked down rather than shouting and saw a plant rubbing the red flowers against the bottom of my foot until the juice wet the sole. Next to me, Thorn and Civet had both ceased struggling and were staring in amazement as the plants also crushed flowers against their feet. And the next thing I knew, the needleweed had soaked my left foot as well.

But Civet was pointing. I turned to see the nee-dleweed by the lake beckoning us to enter.

"Help," I started to yell. Suddenly I was whip-ping toward the lake, passed by one plant to the next. I reached behind my ear to get my staff—though a hoe would have been a better weapon against plants. But even as I was lifting it up, I was suddenly sailing through the air, feet first.

I kept a tight grip on my staff, not wanting to lose it when I hit the water. My feet landed on the lake, but the juice prevented me from feeling anything wet. I crouched and then bounced up again. And when I looked down, I saw that I was standing on top of the water as if it were some kind of transparent sheet.

The next moment Civet and Thorn had been tossed onto the lake as well, where they stood, arms flailing for balance. It took a few seconds for them to get used to the idea of standing on the surface.

"This is amazing," Thorn said.

"No," Civet said. "It's magic." And she looked at the silvery rectangle that still glowed at the bottom of the lake. Well, when adventure invites you like that, it would be impolite to refuse. And I took a step. My foot went under the surface of the water and bounced back up again.

"It's like walking on gelatin," Thorn marveled.

"I prefer traveling by air," I said, and leaped into the sky. I paralleled them as they walked out toward the center of the lake, their feet bouncing along on what seemed like a sheet of black rubber.

Thorn seemed both frightened and thrilled by the new experience, but Civet seemed to move as if in a dream. So when Thorn stopped a few meters from the spot where the door lay glowing beneath the lake, Civet kept walking right past him.

"Wait," I started to say.

Suddenly, it was if the water above the door started to drain. I had time to snatch Thorn up by his collar, but Civet was right in the center of the whirlpool. In vain she stretched out her hands to me, and then she was swept downward out of sight.

Agile as a monkey, Thorn climbed onto my back, and we cautiously somersaulted over the whirlpool. A circular well of air had opened just above the door; a dirty-faced Civet was sitting in the mud at the very threshold of the door. The light was so bright now that it was as if the rectangle had been etched in fire.

"Are you all right?" I called down to her.

"Yes, I think so." Civet's voice echoed hollowly up to us. "I've just got a few bruises."

"Well, don't move. The occupants of this land

weren't saints when they were alive; and I don't expect them to be any better now that they're dead. That could be some kind of trap left over from the war." And looking at my staff, I muttered, "Change." And instantly it grew some ten meters long and as thin as my finger.

Drops of water were still cascading down from the edges of the whirlpool like rain, and the light from below occasionally flashed from the scales of fish that swam too near the well of air.

Civet wiped at her mouth with her hand and then realized that it was only making her face dirtier. "Get me out of here."

"In a jiffy," I called down into the hole cheerfully. "Just pretend you're a sweet-smelling flower." And I started to lower my staff into the well.

Down below us Civet grabbed the lower ring. But just as I started to pull her up, the door suddenly opened with a groan. Light spilled upward, so that the waters of the lake turned as shiny as metal. Startled, Civet let go of my staff.

"Grab hold," I urged her again.

But Civet was staring at the door.

"Hurry."

She started to shuffle toward the door.

"No," I shouted in alarm. "Go back."

"I just want to see what's inside," she said without looking up.

"Come back here," I said.

Civet looked up at us almost in triumph. "I can feel the magic in here stronger than ever."

"Then grab hold," I grunted, and tried to wave the staff at her.

But the memory of her humiliation in the forest still burned inside her. "You don't know what it's like to be without magic. It's an ache. It's a hunger. I won't be helpless again," she declared.

And lifting her head, she marched inside.

When she was out of sight, Thorn punched the air in frustration. "And I thought we could trust her when she said she'd changed and wanted to correct the wrongs she'd done."

"Don't blame yourself. I'm the one who's at fault." I knocked myself on my skull.

I thought of all the mischief she could be up to, for she had stolen the Inland Sea—leaving Shimmer's clan homeless. And then she had tried to destroy a whole city with the sea waters. There was no telling what would happen if she found more magic.

And once again I could hear my master speaking in his gentle but firm way: "Dear me, you seem to have really spilled the dinner pot this time. But let's see what we can salvage. And next time don't be so overconfident."

But this was worse than spoiling his dinner. This was a potential disaster of far greater proportions. "Well"—I chuckled nervously to myself—"you never liked to do things by half."

"What?" Thorn asked.

I squared my shoulders. "I was just trying to work up my nerve."

"We should go back and get the others," Thorn said.

But it was overconfidence that got me into this, and it was overconfidence that would just have to get me out of it—I hoped. Besides, I didn't relish getting a tongue-lashing from Shimmer. She had an unusually imaginative vocabulary even for a dragon.

I set my staff down on the bottom of the lake. It just reached. "It could be too late by then. I'll go down. You go back for the others."

Setting him down on the lake once again, I took a deep breath and jumped from the lake and onto my staff. Folding my legs around the iron shaft, I held on tight as I began to slide down it. As I whizzed downward, I could see the fish and eels as if through a circular window—dark, shadowy shapes darting this way and that in the silvery water like shadows in smoke. Once I was in the air well itself, the stagnant smell of the mud was almost overwhelming. Down below, the light seemed to burn like a silvery fire.

And I had made myself jump right into the middle of it.

CHAPTER SIX

When I landed, I slipped on the mud and wound up flat on my back. It wasn't the most elegant entrance for a hero, and I glanced up to see if my audience had seen me. He had.

Determined to put on a better show, I tried to jump to my feet; but the mud didn't give me enough footing, and I wound up slipping again and landing with a loud squelch right on my fundamentals.

It was back to basics, as my master would say. Or maybe I was just getting old. Holding on to my staff, I finally pulled myself to my feet.

"Have you got hold of the staff?" Thorn asked.

Though I found that a bit puzzling, I waved at him for him to go. "Of course. Better go get Shimmer."

If he saw my paw, he chose to ignore it. "Then

watch out below. Here I come." And jumping on my staff, he began sliding down, with his legs crossed around the iron shaft. So all I could really do was hold the shaft upright and catch him when he reached the bottom.

"Yuck." He lifted one foot and then the other from the clinging, stinking mud.

I reduced my staff to a more manageable size. "We'll both need baths when this is done."

"But maybe not in this lake." Thorn blinked his eyes at the bright light pouring from the doorway.

There was a short corridor whose white marble walls slanted in slightly toward the high ceiling. Mounted along the walls were rows of lamps shaped like men and women with rhino horns. Their mouths were stretched open in agony, and from their lips the silvery light poured like smoke. The walls, floor and ceiling were covered with carvings, and they were all so sad and strange.

Tiger-striped bears burst into flame as they roared, their hearts caged inside their stripes as if behind bars. Elephants with wings fell exhausted from the sky after trying to chase a laughing moon.

Thorn turned in a small circle as he gazed solemnly at the walls. "There isn't one real beast," he said in a low voice to me. The sound echoed sibilantly in the strange corridor like a dozen snakes hissing.

I had been studying the walls at the same time as him. Creatures that were half women and half snakes wept in bamboo groves by the riverbanks. Men who were half butterflies danced their feet bloody before mirrors as they trailed their great wings over the mirror's surface.

"Nor one human," I whispered back. As my words echoed, I had trouble recognizing my own voice.

With a shiver, Thorn hugged himself and rubbed his arms vigorously. "This place gives me the creeps."

I knew what he meant. It was like looking into a book—or more like seeing scenes from plays—but plays performed in a strange, unknown language. And a not very pleasant set of plays either, for everyone seemed to be suffering or in rage. Even if I hadn't been warned about the ancient people of this land, I would have known that they hadn't thought like me.

From up ahead came a clack of pottery. Signing for Thorn to be quiet, I took the lead. Perhaps it was simply moisture coming in from the lake, but the marble felt as slick and pale as the belly of a fish. The sobbing grew louder as we reached the end of the corridor.

There a door opened on a domed chamber whose walls were carved with even angrier and sadder scenes than the corridor. And in the center was a platform on which rested a person—a woman, I thought—in a suit of small lavender-jade rectangles linked together with gold wires. The precious tiles covered even her hands and face; and the sobbing seemed to be coming from behind her jade mask.

Across her forehead was a tiara decorated with phoenixes, fashioned from gold wires and jewels, dancing around a pearl.

But the rest of the chamber—crypt, it seemed to be—looked like a shop after an earthquake. Vases, trunks, baskets lay stacked all around on top of chairs or tables as if people had dumped them wherever it was convenient. Jars as tall as me leaned against one another like drunken sailors. Over on one side was a small chariot that had been disassembled. But dangling from its shafts was a team of toy-sized ceramic horses.

And scattered all around were dollhouses with dolls and miniature furniture. There were palaces and forts and towers and even a star-shaped building. The dolls were of all sorts—from servants with miniature mules to soldiers.

Over to our left Civet was walking on tiptoe in the crypt. With each step she would pause and look around at the objects. Hurriedly she picked up a red vase shaped like a gourd, but she set it down right away. And then she lifted the lid to a basket. It seemed to contain bolts of silk cloth in rainbow colors embroidered with designs. But as she lifted them out, they crumbled into brightly colored dust.

Thorn knelt, fascinated by a miniature boat complete with oarsmen; but he was too afraid to pick it up. "Why are there so many toys?"

I was studying the star-shaped building. "I don't think they're toys," I explained. "I've heard that back in those days, a person was buried with all the things that he or she would need while alive." I jerked a thumb at some of the dolls. "Those are probably servants."

As the light flickered from the pearl on the jade woman's tiara, Civet went over to a wall and began to trace the designs carved into the marble. Frowning in concentration, her lips started to move as if she were slowly reading words.

"Do you understand it?" I whispered.

Her fingers went on exploring the pictures. "It's an old script—one that was almost forgotten even in my own time. But I know this word." She tapped a cloudlike design with wings. "This is the word for wizardry." She looked around eagerly. "There's all sorts of magic in here."

"All the more reason for us to get out of here." I tried to catch her with one of the golden rings at the end of my staff.

But she managed to duck behind some jars. "I'm tired of being treated like so much baggage. I want the magic back that I lost."

Thorn looked at her, puzzled. "But I thought it was just a matter of time before you recovered. You captured us with magic when we followed you into the Weeping Mountain."

"I used up all of my own flooding River Glen. The only real magic I had left came from the mist stone. And that you took away and gave to that worthless worm in the sea."

When Shimmer had captured Civet, she had taken away a magical stone that had allowed Civet to transform herself into a misty form. Shimmer, in turn, had been forced to surrender the stone to her Uncle Sambar, the High King of the dragons.

Suddenly the light began to flicker in the room; and we all turned at the same time toward the platform. The jewel in the tiara was pulsing in rhythm to the sobbing sounds.

Excitedly, Civet stabbed her finger toward the tiara. "But those days are about to change."

"We trusted you." Thorn sounded hurt.

Again I tried to snag her with my ringed staff; but the agile Civet fell onto her back and wriggled behind a pile of furniture. "And I'll keep my word," she grunted. Her head bobbed up for a moment behind the furniture as she got to her feet. "That overgrown worm will get back her sea. But I'll be an even bigger help when I have magic." She ducked as I tried to catch her again. "All I have left is my word. I value it too highly to give it away lightly. You have to trust me."

"It's too dangerous." Shrinking my staff, I stored it behind my ear and started toward her warily. "You don't know what will happen if you put on that tiara."

"I value my neck almost as much as my word. Anyway, a crying ghost can't be very vicious." She rose with the basket that she had just been examining.

Once a Witch, always a Witch, I suppose. I began to slide toward her, intending to grab her and take her forcibly out of the crypt. "Even if we could trust you, the magic here might be tainted and wrong to use."

"This is the first time I've ever really asked anyone for something since I was sent into the river." Hugging the basket to her stomach, she looked young and vulnerable.

"When would-be apprentices come to my master, he always warns them that magic means power, and power can be more addictive than any drug." I got ready to spring at her.

"I won't be stopped when the magic is just within reach." And jerking off the lid of the basket, she threw its contents at me. A basketful of silk handkerchiefs seemed to float in the air toward me. But when they hit my face, they collapsed instantly into dust. And then I was coughing and trying to breathe in a cloud of what had once been costly fabric. For a moment I couldn't even see.

"I mean you no harm," I heard her say. "I swear that I serve a good cause. My friend and I have great need. We are upon a hard quest and are being pursued by many enemies. Might I borrow your jewel?

I will return it as soon as possible. And when I do, I swear I will find out your name so that others will remember your generosity as well."

And even with my eyes blinded with dust, I could sense the jewel brightening as if in welcome.

"Don't." I tried to wipe the dust from my eyes, but my paws were now as filthy as the rest of me. I bumped right into a jar, tipping it over so it crashed on the floor.

Thorn took one of my arms. "Let me clean your eyes."

With his sleeve he carefully wiped my eyes until I could at least see a blurry room. Civet was bowing her head to the woman in the jade suit.

"Get away from there," I warned her.

But she was already climbing up to the platform. Immediately, the sobbing stopped. Even as I jumped into the air, Civet bowed her head once again. "May I?" she said to the woman in the suit.

And the pearl flared even brighter, so that the whole suit seemed to glow and I could see the shadowy skeleton within.

I was still in midair as Civet said, "Thank you." Stretching out her fingers, she tried to take the tiara. But at her first touch, the jewel filled the room with a light so brilliant that for a moment I was blinded again.

My paws groped for her, but I went sailing over her head to crash into another pile of furniture. Blinking my eyes, I whirled around and thought I saw that the light was already fading to a soft glow. "Don't!" I shouted.

"I have to." With trembling fingers, she reached out toward the tiara.

I leaped as she began easing the tiara from the jade-covered head. Triumphantly she raised it over her own head. "Now to find out what it can do."

"At least wait and read more of the writing in here," I begged. "We have to make sure that the owner has a good heart." I tried to snatch the tiara from her hands, but Civet ducked behind the platform.

As soon as I landed on the floor, I bounced into the air again in a backward somersault—just in time for an upside-down view as Civet set the tiara upon her head.

Suddenly, her hands dropped to her sides. "Oh!" she said in a high, surprised voice. "Oh, everything's so clear now."

I landed just in front of her. "What's clear?"

[67]

But the next instant her head had snapped back. Her eyes widened and her mouth fell open. "No!" she gasped.

I wanted to go to her, but it was as if my feet were glued to the floor. "Are you all right?"

Thorn came up to me. "Let us help you."

But as she slowly turned, spurts of brightly colored dust rose from her robes.

"What's wrong?" Thorn slid back a step.

However, Civet only turned faster, her feet slapping against the floor. She raised her arms away from her sides. And as she turned, her sleeves and hem billowed outward. Dust rose from her clothes like flocks of ghostly parrots. And the quicker she spun, the more the pearl glowed. I glanced at the design of dancing phoenixes upon the tiara. In the bright light cast by the pearl, I could see that the phoenixes had human faces.

As Civet's feet slapped out a kind of music upon the floor, Thorn looked at me. "What do we do now?"

CHAPTER SEVEN

As Civet danced out into the middle of the crypt, I shook my head at Thorn. "I was afraid something like this would happen." I looked back at the now-quiet jade suit. "Back in those days, a lot of the magicians were cut from the same cloth as the Nameless One."

Thorn gaped at the dancing Civet as she scattered dolls and broke vases in her mad, desperate spinning. "What's going to happen to her?"

"She's been taken over"—I nodded toward the sorceress in the jade suit—"by that other person's spirit." Then I looked grimly at the walls for some clue about how to help her; but only Civet knew how to read that script.

A loud sob from within the tomb yanked our attention back to Civet. She had dropped to her knees. "Fire!" Wrapping her arms around herself, she leaned forward as if in sudden pain. "No, no, the flames."

"Maybe Shimmer can read the walls," Thorn suggested. "You go get her. I'll stay and watch."

I glanced at the woman in the suit. "I wouldn't dare leave either of you alone in this place."

Thorn seemed glad of company. "They're bound to miss us sooner or later and come looking."

My head ached when I thought of all the self-righteous sermonizing I would have to listen to from that dragon. "Maybe we can fix the trouble on our own," I said hopefully.

Civet stared at me crazily, as if she were seeing right through me. "The Evil waits. Why do you just stand there?"

I watched as she rose and began to dance again, feet smashing through a model palace.

"We have to break that spell," I said, "before she hurts herself."

Thorn glanced uncomfortably at the woman in the suit. "It only started when she put on the tiara. Maybe if we got it off her head, we'd break the spell."

I tugged my cap tighter about my head. "No sooner said than done." With a determined spring, I leaped into the air toward her. But I had hardly landed in front of her when Civet jerked her arms up stiffly like a stick puppet. "Fool! Do not try to stop me. The world must be warned."

Though there were several meters between her and me, it was as if a giant hand picked me up and threw me against the chariot. The wood shattered underneath me.

As I lay in the wreckage, I struggled to open one eye and looked over at Thorn. Between us, the ceramic horses were prancing from the shafts of the chariot. "Well," I asked, "any other ideas? I think that I've just demonstrated that the direct approach won't work." I added with a wheeze, "I, for one, am open to new suggestions."

Civet was kneeling, her shoulders shaking as she wept uncontrollably. "The great work is unfinished. The task must be completed. But who will dare? Who?"

Careful to keep away from her, Thorn made his way over to me and helped me to sit up. "She's not going to let us near her. Could we knock off the tiara?"

"We'd probably knock her head off too." I took the needle from behind my ear. "But I've been known to scratch the itchy back of a gnat at three meters."

As a precaution, I motioned for him to hide behind a pile of furniture; and when he was safely hidden, I whispered, "Change."

The instant I felt the staff grow in my hand, I jumped up and swung my weapon toward the tiara. But Civet threw up a hand, and it was as if I'd hit an invisible wall. "Fool. The Great Evil waits for you. He prays for your coming."

And suddenly I was flying backward, through several jars that cracked beneath me, before I slammed the far wall.

As I slid down toward the floor, Thorn peeked out at me from behind the furniture. "No," I groaned. "I don't think that's going to work either."

He came over to me on his hands and knees. "I've got another idea."

"I was afraid of that," I moaned, and pulled myself into a sitting-up position. My staff lay about three meters away, where I had dropped it. It might as well have been a kilometer away for all the good it did me. Civet was now suspicious of my every move.

It took Thorn a while to reach me because he had to freeze each time Civet looked at him.

When he sat down, he touched his head against mine so he could speak in the lowest of whispers. "Once there were these rich travelers who stayed at the inn. My old master, Knobby, was eager to make a good impression, so he had me dress up and wait on them. But I spilled wine on the lady's pearl necklace, and she became quite upset. She said her pearls were ruined now because the wine would eat at them." He winced at the memory. "After the beating, I couldn't sit down for a week."

"That must have been some vintage," I grunted.

"No, no," Thorn insisted, "the lady said that the wine is like an acid."

I was still skeptical. "But a pearl?"

"We call pearls gems, but it's not as if they're mineral like emeralds or rubies." Thorn rubbed the tips of two fingers together. "After all, every pearl begins when a grain of sand gets inside an oyster, and the oyster starts to coat the sand."

I looked around me. Rice and wine were spilling from the jars that I had broken. "If we could dissolve the pearl, we might free her from the spell." I began to study the intact jars intently. "Maybe one of those has some wine that's still magically sealed."

Thorn drew up a bony knee and rested his chin on it. "But it would take too long to spill wine on her."

"And," I mused, "it's not like she's going to let us stick her head into the nearest wine jar."

At that moment we heard Shimmer's voice coming from above the lake. "Botheration! I can't find any place to land."

Right then I was glad even of her help—though I would have to pay for it later. Cupping my hands around my mouth to amplify my voice, I shouted, "You could if you shrank." I added before Shimmer could reply, "I know, I know, a dragon princess has to be a proper size. But this is an emergency."

A moment later, reduced to the size of a cat, Shimmer swept in from the corridor into the crypt itself.

Civet's hands batted at the air as she stared at some invisible horror. "Fire," she cried. "Fire everywhere. Help me. Help me. Why won't you help me?" Suddenly she wrapped her arms around herself as if instantly cold. "And the Void waits. The Great Void."

"Cheerful customer, isn't she?" I asked as Shimmer settled down on my shoulder. Quickly I filled her in on what had happened.

She stamped her hindpaws on me, forgetting about how sharp her claws were. "I knew we couldn't trust her."

"If you're going to perch on me, treat your landlord with more respect." I started to raise my paw

[74]

to brush Shimmer off. Instantly, Civet got ready to zap me. With an apologetic smile, I quickly lowered my paw.

"Look," I said from the corner of my mouth, "you can save the scoldings for later. Right now we have to get the tiara off her head. Or find some other weakness." I rolled my eyes at the walls. "Can you read any of this?"

Shimmer studied the crypt. "It's an old script that I never had a chance to learn."

Civet's head sank back upon her shoulders. "And he shall drive all before him." And slowly her hand rose and pointed at us.

"Then why don't you be a good girl and take the tiara off?" I began to get to my feet; but with a flap of her hand, Civet knocked both Shimmer and me down onto our backs.

"He shall sit with the great kings and queens of this world," she said, and her finger slowly swung toward Thorn.

Stunned, Thorn spread his fingers across his chest. "Me?"

Civet kept pointing at him as she got to her feet. "Dragon and human, skin or scale—all shall bow to his power."

"She's gone crazy," Thorn said.

Shimmer, though, called softly, "Go along with her. Distract her." And she crawled backward.

Civet took a step toward Thorn. "And he shall be eternal."

Thorn was too stunned to say anything, but I whispered to him, "Play along."

The boy squirmed uncomfortably as Civet continued toward him. "And . . . unh . . . just how am I supposed to do that?"

But she was too caught up in her vision to pay attention to him. "All shall kneel."

"Keep her occupied," Shimmer's tiny voice whispered in my ear.

I didn't dare turn around to check, but I was pretty sure that Shimmer had shrunk herself down even more. Licking my lips, I shook my head at Civet. "You don't really mean him," I said in my gentlest, least-threatening voice.

"Flee. Flee. All shall flee before him." Civet spread her arms. "But there will be no hiding from his power." And she glared at Thorn. "Because it is he who will loose the Evil once again."

CHAPTER EIGHT

Just then something about the size of a small bird darted into the air. It moved so fast that it was a green blur, but I would have bet anything it was Shimmer.

"Why would I help this . . . this evil?" Thorn began to babble. "And anyway, I'm just a boy. I don't have any power."

She was right in front of him now. "He who has the power to release also has the power to destroy."

The next instant Shimmer banked in the room and zoomed at the back of Civet's head. But perhaps Civet heard something, because she whirled around and slapped at the air.

Again, though they were still several meters apart, it was as if Civet had swatted Shimmer. The dragon went tumbling head over paws to plop on the floor.

"Shimmer!" I said, and scrambled to my feet. But

before I could make a dive for my staff, Civet had raised her other hand and knocked me back against the wall.

"Puny fools. You need me. Why are you trying to drive me away?" Civet's fingers curled into fists, and she raised them as if she were going to strike at us.

"No," Thorn shouted. He didn't believe her crazy prophecies for one moment; but he seemed to have some hold on her.

She stopped and looked respectfully over her shoulder at him.

"If you want me to help you, you have to explain about my power." And taking a deep breath, Thorn slowly got to his feet. At each moment I expected him to be knocked down with one of her invisible blows.

"Without me," she moaned, "you will free a great evil."

Shimmer and I were lying where we had fallen. Desperately I looked at the jars, hunting for one with wine. They came in all sizes, from ones as round as pumpkins to others as slim as pickles; but I couldn't make head or tail of the writing.

But leave it to the ever-resourceful Thorn to come up with something else. "All right," he said, "if you say so. But we should start the right way. Let's pour out a gift to the spirits of the earth." Thorn pivoted and pointed to a big, broad bowl. "We need their support, or we're bound to make a mistake."

Civet seemed to pull herself back from someplace within herself. "Yes, of course, you're right."

She went to a jar that was as red and round as a grape, and with a finger she broke the seal. "Here."

With that as a clue, I looked around the room, but to my dismay I didn't see another jar like that. When Thorn glanced at me, I gave a slight shake of my head.

Somehow Thorn managed not to panic. With his sleeve, he cleaned out the bowl, and he coolly picked up the opened jar; and though it was heavy, he managed to tilt it so that sparkling red wine spilled into the bowl. The tomb quickly filled with an aroma sweet as summer. If the scent was any proof, the wine was as fresh as when it had been stored in here—as if the magic had worked at least on this jar.

"Your spirits are that thirsty?" Civet asked, puzzled.

"Yes, they're very thirsty." Thorn poured the entire jar into the bowl. When the bowl was filled to the brim, Thorn knelt beside it. "Now we must bow our heads and ask their blessing."

Civet frowned suspiciously. "I never heard of this."

Thorn licked his lips nervously. "You've been in here a long time."

"Perhaps you're right." With a sigh, Civet bowed her head over the bowl.

Instantly Thorn threw himself at her and shoved her head into the bowl. Gasping, she managed to raise her face out of the wine. "Fool, you must let me stay in this body, or you will commit a great sin in your ignorance."

"Your time is finished. Let Civet live her own life," Thorn grunted. And with a desperate push, he forced her face back into the wine.

Her hands flew up angrily. But then she held them there, frozen. I don't know what it was. Maybe the wine had already begun to dissolve the pearl, so it had started to lose its hold over Civet.

At any rate, this wasn't time for sitting and speculating. I jumped up at the same time as Shimmer rose into the air. However, Thorn had already snatched the tiara from Civet's head. Grabbing her hair, he pulled her head up. Civet gasped for air, wine spilling down her face onto her robe.

As Thorn submerged the tiara within the bowl, he apologized to her. "I'm sorry for doing that, but it was the only way I could think of to get that thing off—"

Panting, Civet nodded her head dumbly. Shimmer darted over and hovered centimeters by her ear. "He should have let you drown," she scolded. "Of all the hare-brained schemes—"

"Look," Thorn cried.

I stared down at the fumes rising from the bowl. "Whether the wine's powerful or the pearl is sensitive, we know that they don't mix."

Leaving the tiara in the bowl, Thorn ripped a patch from his shirt and held it out to Civet. "What was the 'great work' that was left unfinished?"

Civet wiped her face slowly. "The images came so fast that it was hard to understand them." She lowered the now-damp square of cotton and stared at Thorn. "But I saw you." She paused, and there was almost awe in her voice. "And humans and dragons bowed to you."

"You were out of your head," Shimmer snapped.

Suddenly Civet looked tired and worn out. "I saw what I saw."

I retrieved my staff, taking comfort in its familiar weight. "What about that evil you talked about?"

Civet wrinkled her forehead. "I don't know. The images were all so strange, and . . . and trying to grasp one was like trying to grab snowflakes. They just melted away. But I did see . . ." Her voice trailed off.

"What?" I demanded urgently.

She wadded up the cloth and threw it away. "I was burning," she said softly.

I poked cautiously at the tiara in the bowl, but it was simply a gold frame now. "They were just fantasies—all from this weird pearl." I held the tiara up for her to see. "But they're all gone now."

I froze as a high, thin wail came from within the jade suit. And suddenly the suit itself collapsed, the tiles falling upon one another with loud clacking noises. A basket in the corner suddenly disintegrated into a heap of dust. The next moment a chair crumpled into a pile of sticks.

Cracks zigzagged across the ceiling as swiftly as lightning. "We've got to get out of here," I said, and dumped the tiara back into the bowl. But the spell preserving the wine had also failed, and there was now only a thick syrup inside the bowl. As soon as the tiara landed, it tumbled into a tangle of gold wires.

Shimmer hovered over Thorn and flapped her wings like a worried hen. "Come on."

But he had already taken Civet's elbow and helped her to stand up. I got on the other side to support her. As furniture and tapestries fell apart, we made our way back to the corridor.

We were near the entrance when the dome crashed down into the crypt and the dust came rolling out in a blinding cloud. Shimmer was already hovering outside. The watery walls of the air well were beginning to whirl faster and faster. "Hurry."

Letting go of Civet, I took my staff and held it perpendicular to the bottom of the lake. "Hang on to her and grab hold of the top loop," I said to Thorn.

As soon as he had done so, I squatted down on my haunches and gripped the lower half. "Change," I shouted.

Instantly, the staff began to grow taller; and as the top loop shot upward, it jerked Civet and Thorn from their feet. Legs dangling, they soared up toward safety.

Shimmer buzzed around in an anxious circle before the entrance. "I wish we had time to read the corridor walls. They might tell us where the Smith is."

"Too late," I grunted as I held on to the staff. "They're collapsing."

Even as we watched, cracks appeared on the corridor walls and chunks began to bounce down upon the floor.

"The air well's begining to give way," Thorn shouted down to us.

"Get off," I said, and swung the staff so that it tilted toward the surface. The next moment, Civet and Thorn had let go and dropped toward the lake.

"Race you," Shimmer cried, and darted like a hummingbird up the air well.

With one paw on my staff, I began leaping up its length. The opening up above looked much narrower; and all around me the water was spiraling around so fast that I could see nothing beyond it. Below me the doorway crashed inward, and water spilled into the spot where we had been standing.

Thorn and Civet stood on top of the water at a safe distance from the whirlpool that was forming; and Shimmer was hovering above their heads

Sitting down on the air, I changed my staff to the size of a needle and stored it away. "I knew I shouldn't have eaten so much. You wouldn't have won otherwise."

Below me, the lake boiled and bubbled until there

was a sudden burst of light and the lake was dark once more.

When I joined them, Shimmer panted, "I'd change myself back to my proper size, but I'm too tired."

I twisted my head to look at her. "But I thought lizard size was the right one."

Shimmer might have been too tired to perform magic, but she wasn't too tired to dart her head out and bite me on my ear. Dragon fangs, even small ones, are pretty sharp—as I found out.

CHAPTER NINE

Indigo was fairly dancing with impatience. "What happened?" she demanded as we stepped off the lake onto the shore itself.

But Shimmer hovered before Civet. "I thought I could trust you."

I myself had seen Civet destroy an entire city with the sea she had stolen from Shimmer's clan; and she would have slaughtered all its inhabitants if I hadn't tricked her. However, at that moment she seemed more like some rebellious teenager. But then, without magic she was just that. "You don't understand. I would have used the magic *for* you—not against you."

Shimmer gave a snort. "What makes you think I would believe you again?"

Civet clenched her fists. "I didn't ask to be sent to the King Within the River. And perhaps it was

t this stuff." Even
nch of the plants.
n useful." As she
glanced at Civet.

vay from her sides.
he lake, which was
ler. "But not here."
uneventfully, and
he mysterious lake.
eland, though once
ids that Shimmer
landscape was more
o when we saw the
liately called to us.
want to get rid of

m Shimmer's back.
ish leaped from the

hung low near the
we make camp?"
a leisurely descent.
er fish has to clean

iverbank in an area

wrong to seek revenge. But I'm trying to make up for it now."

Shimmer smiled grimly. "I can't leave you, so you'll have to come with us. But consider yourself a captive." She raised a paw with her claws extended, each as sharp as a dagger. "And if you try to escape, it's all over for you."

I'll give Civet this much. She didn't even flinch. "I know what I am doing. Do you?" And she gave a sad little laugh.

Shimmer lowered her paw uncertainly. "You've been warned." And then she rounded on Thorn. "I don't expect any common sense out of this ape. But I thought I could count on you to keep these two in line." She waved a paw at Indigo. "Indigo has more sense in her little fingernail than you have in your whole brain."

And sweeping around, she stamped up the shore toward the fire, whose coals still gleamed like red eyes.

"What happened?" Indigo asked helplessly as Shimmer strode past.

Poor Thorn was left staring after Shimmer and having to swallow all his excuses.

Desperately, Indigo turned to him. "What happened?"

"Leave me alone," he snapped.

[87]

The hurt and frustration were so plain i
that I tried to talk to him. "Thorn—" I l

But he didn't answer. He didn't even tui
to look at me. He just stood there, still ga
lessly at Shimmer's angrily swishing tail.

Giving up on Thorn and me, Indigo
Civet and took in Civet's hair, which was
together now that the wine had changed
"What happened to you? You look like
dragged through a mudhole. Where did
How come you were walking on the wate

Civet took one of her sticky strands of
examined it. "I'm . . . I'm not sure. It all ş
a bad dream."

Slapping a leg in frustration, Indigo ro
me. "Somebody talk to me."

I glanced at the stricken Thorn, wanting
him feel better. "It was really thanks to T
any of us got out." But, too modest to bra
remained silent, so I told Indigo what had h
down in the crypt. "It was Thorn who sav
from being possessed."

Civet spun on her heel and looked sh
Thorn. "Is this true?"

"Monkey and Shimmer were there too,
said uncomfortably.

there was something funny abo
so, she stooped and seized a b
"Still, this juice might come
yanked up another handful, sh
"You should wash up."

Civet held her sticky sleeves a
"I should." She glanced back at
dark once again, and gave a shud

The rest of the night passed
dawn saw us starting away from
We flew over more desolate was
we passed over a set of mou
thought had once been a city. The
monotonous than threatening, s
silver ribbon of a river, it imme

"Me for a wash," I called. "
this stinking mud."

"Please do," Indigo sniffed fro

The dragon circled lower as
water. "Fresh fish, too."

I nodded to the sun, which
horizon. "It's getting late. Shal

Shimmer had already begun
"And the one who catches few
the catch."

So we made camp near the

sheltered by a ridge of soil. While the rest of us washed the lake mud from ourselves and our clothes, Indigo began to break up a dead bush for a fire.

Civet and Thorn were a bit more decorous, kneeling on the riverbank to wash themselves and their clothes. But I simply threw myself in the river and splashed about noisily.

"Have a care," Shimmer scolded me from the bank. "You don't want to scare the fish." She made no attempt to hide the fact that she was watching Civet.

As Civet knelt in a long white shift, she began to wash out her long hair. Absently, like any other young girl, she began to hum. Thorn, who was shivering as he rubbed the cold water on his limbs, glanced over at her. "That's a nice tune. What's it called?"

Civet laughed as she began to scrub at her ragged robe. "I've forgotten, and the people who might remember are long since dust." Her robe, its bright colors showing again, trailed like a ragged flag in the river currents. "But it was very popular when I was young."

She seemed so sad right then that I pulled myself up on the riverbank and began to shake off the excess water. "Hum a few bars, and perhaps I'll remember," I offered.

She hesitated, then shook her head fiercely. "Those days are gone, and there's no use pretending. We have to look ahead." She looked at the barrens. "We mustn't let this happen to the rest of the world."

"What do you care about the world?" Shimmer demanded skeptically.

"I lost something beautiful once—an entire forest." Using her reflection on the river water, Civet spread her hair out to dry upon her back. The cloth of her turban snaked back and forth over a broad rock like a giant flattened snake. "I thought I could return to the forest I knew as a girl, but over the years it had been destroyed. I won't let that happen again."

I think she felt guilty over the harm she had done to Shimmer and her clan—though Civet would not admit it.

I thought Thorn sensed it too. He looked reproachfully at Shimmer. "It's possible for people to change."

"And maybe horses will fly and Monkey will be serious for once," Shimmer sniffed. "But I doubt it."

Civet suffered the insult meekly. Her experience within the crypt seemed to have shaken her. "Perhaps," she said quietly to the dragon, "the hatred will burn out inside you as it has in me."

Back at the campsite, we found that Indigo had a

little fire going. At her request, Shimmer used some of her magic to change some rocks into pots and other useful containers.

"I'll need a little jar with a string, too," Indigo said. "After dinner, I'll boil down the needleweed. That juice might come in handy."

Pleased, Shimmer nodded her head. "Well, aren't you the clever one?"

Civet laid her robe on a bush so the fire could dry it out. "We should find some large logs."

"Yes, make yourself useful," Shimmer said, and nodded to Thorn. "Go with her. And," she added sternly, "don't let her out of your sight."

As the two of them left, I hunkered down on the bank and took my staff from behind my ear. "Aren't you going to make a fishing pole for yourself?"

She raised a paw. "I don't need your newfangled inventions."

"I hope you like cleaning fish," I chuckled, but I could smell some kind of dragonish trick. Draping my tail over my shoulder, I plucked some hairs from it. Spitting on them, I changed them into a long string. "You," I suggested as I tied my line to my staff, "might have a kind word every now and then for Thorn, you know."

Shimmer stretched out her limbs until her joints

popped as she sought to limber herself up for our new contest. "He knows how I feel about him."

Surreptitiously I plucked out another handful of hairs, but I changed only one into a hook. "But he hears you praising Indigo all the time."

Shimmer puffed as she did a massive series of knee bends. "I've explained my reasons to him. The poor girl has led such a hard life that she needs encouragement."

"She's not the only one who's had it rough," I pointed out. "Thorn has also had hard times." Even harder since he met her, I added to myself, though I didn't say it.

"True, but at least he was among his own kind," Shimmer said stiffly.

I thought of Shimmer's years of exile among humans. "You think of her as a human version of you."

Shimmer, for all of her years of wandering the world disguised as a human beggar, was still a princess at heart. She didn't like to be told when she was wrong. "Mind your own business," she snapped, and looked away from me pointedly.

Taking advantage of the opportunity she had presented to me, I bent my head over my lap and changed the other hairs into tiny monkeys no bigger than fingernails. To them I gave whispered instructions. But almost as an afterthought, I sent the last two after Thorn and Civet.

Shimmer had taken up a position ten meters upstream. "Ready?" she asked, crouching.

"Wait, wait." I finally found a worm and baited my hook. "All right."

"Onetwothree—start." Shimmer instantly struck at a shadowy shape in the water, and the next moment she was scooping a fish onto the bank, where it lay flopping and panting.

With all her big teeth, Shimmer's smile was an awesome spectacle. "I've got you this time, you little fur bag. This is one contest I can't lose."

"Oh deary me, oh deary me," I pretended to moan, but actually it was my signal to my children. From the corner of my eye, I saw the other little monkeys leave their hiding places among the weeds along the riverbank and slip into the water quietly.

"You have to get up pretty early to beat a dragon at fishing," Shimmer said, laughing, and scooped another fish onto the bank.

Shimmer managed to get a third fish before one team of little monkeys had taken up their positions underwater. And then I felt a tug as the other team of monkeys caught a fish and wrestled it onto my hook. "I got one," I yelled, and hauled it onto the bank.

"Beginner's luck," Shimmer snapped, and stared at the water intently.

She didn't say anything as I caught another and then a third. But when I hooked a fourth a moment later, she stomped her paws in the dirt. "Botheration. Where are the fish?"

I chuckled. "It took all this time for them to hear that I've arrived for a visit."

And while the first team of monkeys kept fish away from Shimmer, I kept pulling in one fish after another until I was ankle deep in silvery, flopping bodies. "I think," I finally announced, "that I'm going to stop fishing. My arms are tired." And I lifted my hook from the water as a signal to the other monkeys to return.

"Thunderation." Shimmer slapped the water in frustration with her tail. "Where did all the fish go?"

While she was busy cursing and punishing the river, my little monkeys slipped out of the water. Changing them back quickly into hairs, I stuck them back onto my tail. Only then did I begin to untie the string from my staff. "I say, old chum, will you give me a hand with my fishy haul?"

Shimmer swung her head around to say something insulting when she saw my hook. "How could you catch fish without any bait?"

I had been so busy hauling in one fish after another that I hadn't noticed that the worm had fallen off the hook. "Well, imagine that. I guess I really don't know." I flashed her my best imitation of a broad, dragonish smile. "I suppose it was such an honor to be hauled in by me that they just lined up to hang themselves on my hook."

She craned her long neck around to look behind me. "And why is part of your tail wet?"

I changed the line and hook back into hairs that I restored to my tail. "Haven't you heard? It's an old monkey custom to dip our tail in a river when we've won a great victory."

Shimmer glowered at me. "If I could figure out how you tricked me, I'd dip your head in the river."

I shrank my staff and tucked it behind my ear. "In the meantime, my big green fish cleaner, you can give me a hand carrying our dinner back to the fire."

When we got back to the camp, we found that Indigo already had a roaring fire going. She made satisfying exclamations as we dumped fish onto the dirt. But Thorn was as somber as an undertaker, and Civet was sitting with her back to the big fire—as if she were afraid of the leaping flames.

"Are you still having nightmares about the lake?" I asked her with calculated kindness.

For the moment she looked simply like someone lost and frightened. "They were too real to be nightmares. They were visions."

"If they were visions," I suggested, "then they were only visions of what might be. Do you remember anything more about the evil that's waiting for us?"

She shook her head slowly. "Just . . . just the flames."

As Civet sat there silently, still afraid to look at the fire, Indigo went over to help Shimmer clean the fish. However, I'll give the dragon this much: She insisted on honoring our bet.

"Though," she added with typical afterthought, "honor might be the least part of our contest."

Her claws were perfect instruments for gutting and scraping the fish, and Indigo was cooking them as fast as Shimmer cleaned them. And a full belly made even Shimmer eventually forget her terrible defeat.

However, I was curious about what had made Thorn so sober. As the others settled down around the fire, Civet made a point of lying down just on the edge of the light—as if the sight of the flames still disturbed her.

Patting my stomach and saying I wanted to work off my dinner, I went into the bushes, where my two little monkeys were waiting. When I held out my paws, each jumped onto one.

Normally I don't like to eavesdrop on people; but I do a good many things that I don't like. Dragons can talk all they like about honor, because they're moving forts with hides tough as steel and claws and fangs sharp as daggers. Monkeys have always been small and fragile, so we have to depend mainly upon our wits.

"Did you hear them?" I asked my little monkeys.

The one on my left paw piped up. "Yes. I'll be Thorn."

And the one on my right chirped, "And I'll be Civet." And it turned to the one on my left. "Thank you for saving me."

The little monkey on my left shrugged in imitation of Thorn. "It was for all of us."

"There was a bond between us even before this," Civet had said, "for I shared my memories with you there in my mountain when I had captured you and Shimmer."

Thorn had shuddered. Apparently they weren't very pleasant memories. "I remember how you suffered with your husband."

"But I can see now that our destinies are intertwined," she had gone on. "There is a terrible evil waiting for us. And it may be that only we can stop it. And so you must be prepared to meet your fate, as I must."

"Those were just crazy dreams," Thorn had insisted.

"There is a force that all magic taps," she had said. "It can work for good. It can work for evil. That is up to the person who calls upon it. But not everyone can; and sometimes it leaves, as it has me."

"Do you miss it very much?" Thorn had asked.

"The power was nice, but there was also a kind of awareness. It was as if . . ." She had paused while she hunted for the right words. "It was being more aware of the world." She had nodded her head as she came to the right realization. "It was like being able to see colors when everyone else is colorblind."

"Perhaps it will come back," Thorn had suggested.

"Perhaps." She looked sad. "But after last night, I think that door is closed to me."

Thorn had looked puzzled. "But you worked

magic without the mist stone. Why couldn't you work magic when we met those soldiers?"

"It's gone, all gone." She had looked at Thorn intently. "And yet I know now that there is some purpose for having me travel with you. It isn't to help the dragon, but you."

"I'm no warrior," Thorn had protested. "I'm only an ex-serving boy."

"Your fate is far better than mine," Civet had informed him. "Be prepared to accept it."

"But you already drowned and changed, so how can you die?" Thorn had demanded.

"I can be destroyed," she had said. "Even so, I won't leave this world easily. And yet"—the little monkey smiled sadly in imitation of the former witch—"if that is what it takes to save the world, then I will do what I have to."

"Here's a log," Thorn had said, as if he had wanted to change the subject. As the little monkey squatted down, I stopped him.

"You've done well, my children." And I changed them back into hairs and returned them to my tail. Perhaps Shimmer was wrong about Civet. I had a good deal to think over.

CHAPTER TEN

By afternoon of the next day, we found ourselves in the foothills of the mountains that they call the Desolate Mountains. The river exploded through the gap between the steep-sided hills. Wind and water had eroded the soft limestone into spires and spikes and shaped the slabs into odd shapes that I could almost make out—but not quite. They looked like a sculptor's rough experiments—or real statues that were melting away.

And the cold mountain water foamed and roared around the rocks. Even the spray along the river-banks was chilly. The soil on the riverbank was black with moisture, and beads of water dripped from the branches of the cinnamon trees.

Shimmer paused grandly and sniffed the air. "Ah," she sighed. "There's nothing quite like the smell of wet cinnamon trees."

I couldn't resist poking fun at yet another dragonish affectation. Tilting my head back with exaggerated elegance, I snorted at the air. "Unless it's the smell of sage on a high mountain desert after the rain."

The pompous lizard didn't even realize when she was being teased. But then she hated to be outdone when it came to affairs of the snout. Raising her head in a superior fashion, she began to say, "Or willows blossoming on a hot day by—"

"Really." Civet wiped her sleeve across her damp face. "If either of you lifted your noses any higher, you would drown."

"I try to share my wisdom with you," Shimmer grumbled, "and look at the thanks I get." She squatted down. "Well, climb on board."

I arranged it so that I was carrying Civet; and as we flew low over the hills, a breeze blew through the cinnamon trees beneath us and the needles rustled. I felt her shift on my back, and I glanced behind me to make sure she was all right. To my surprise she was looking almost wistfully down at the fir trees. "Are you all right?" I asked.

She gave me a slight smile. "I'm not going to get airsick, if that's what you're afraid of."

I knew a little of her background from Thorn and

Shimmer, so I thought I understood her wistful look. She was probably thinking of the vanished forest she had once loved. "Did you miss the trees when you were trapped under the river?"

She glanced at me and then back at the forest. "Yes," she said as if she were embarrassed at having admitted even that much.

She was a strange creature in her own way. Her conversation last night with Thorn had been the longest I'd heard from her—as if she were some little volcano that erupted in words only once in a while.

But then, perhaps, I might be the same way if my own family had sent me as a sacrifice to the river spirit. Poor creature, she was barely an adult when that happened. No wonder her whole life, after her magical transformation, had been taken up with revenge.

I said casually, "I was once imprisoned under a mountain. I could see the sky, hear the birds; but there was nothing I could do until my master came and rescued me."

In some ways trying to speak to the real Civet was like trying to coax a small animal out of hiding. "Then you understand how precious the world can be."

"Yes," I said as we flew into Cloud Pass. An old

caravan track rose away from the river, and we followed it as it wound through a gap in the mountains to the forested tops, where the cinnamon trees gave way to fir.

"I can smell the fir trees already," I said, sniffing the air.

She was silent for a time. Who knows what effort it took to overcome her shyness. "Couldn't we walk among the trees for a little while?"

I glanced at Shimmer but knew she would never agree. "I'm sorry," I said regretfully. "It's faster flying."

"Of course," she said in a small voice—as if she thought this would be her last time to smell them.

I hated to see her withdraw once again. "You know," I ventured, "I knew a prophet once. He said that visions were always tricky things. It's very hard to tell what *will* be from what *could* be. That was always his excuse for forgetting his umbrella when it rained."

The ancient caravan road still paralleled the river, and the spray in the gorge was rising about us so much that it seemed to be raining all the time. "I saw what I saw," she spluttered. "And so I intend to enjoy what time I have."

I blinked my eyes against the drops pelting my

face. "That's not a bad idea in general. And when you find yourself living so long that even my fur is gray, try to keep that same attitude."

She didn't answer, staying out of reach in that sad, hidden part of herself.

The mountains that formed the Desolate Mountains were so old that they made even me feel young. And they were so big that Shimmer with all her dragon's strength and size seemed like an insect.

Tall fir trees stood shrouded in snow like white spikes. The snow-covered ridges gleamed like old bones, and the wrinkled sides looked like dusty leather wings folded down over the heads of slumbering monsters. Below us the river was a distant murmur, rising from a hole within a mountain just below a cave along the caravan track.

Most everyone spoke in a hushed voice, as if afraid of waking the mountains—everyone, that is, except Civet. True to her new philosophy, she was trying to take pleasure even in this rugged wilderness. "That's called Egg Mountain, but I really don't see why. Do you?"

Indigo's hair, still greased into blue spikes, vibrated in the wind. "I'm glad one of us is enjoying this tour."

The long sleeves of Civet's jacket flapped in the

wind of our passage. "It's like going back to the beginning of time. They say that this was once the kingdom of the Nameless One—as fair a realm as any in the world; but in the fight it was warped by the Serpent Lady into these mountains; and Cloud Pass itself was made by the Unicorn dancing in celebration of their victory before the Master of Animals vanished from this world."

"Personally I wouldn't mind sitting on a beach right now," Shimmer puffed. The air itself was growing thinner, so we all had to breathe deeper. But the thin air also meant more work for Shimmer, since she had to beat her wings twice as fast.

When we rounded the mountain, we saw the river once again as it plunged into the mountain.

Suddenly, from somewhere far away, I thought I heard the sound of a horn, the notes stretched out by the distance until they were almost more like wails. "What's that?" I asked.

Shimmer banked sharply to the left and then to the right as the mountain pass doubled back on itself. "It's just the wind," she said.

"No, I heard it too," Thorn chimed in. He gripped the strap of the gourd, which he was carrying.

Shimmer twisted her long neck around to look at me. "Could it be the Smith's guards?"

I shook my head. "The guards there don't use horns. They don't even breathe."

In the meantime I'd been looking this way and that. Below us the snow-covered caravan track wound along like a gleaming sheet of cotton, and farther below, the river shone like a silver ribbon. And the stone walls of the pass soared emptily up beyond us on either side, snowdrifts edging the walls like white fur. Suddenly it seemed as if a white head peered over the edge.

"Up there." I pointed excitedly.

But even as the others leaned back to look, the head seemed to unravel into thin threads of snow that vanished as I watched.

"It was just a breeze whipping up the snow," Indigo said, exasperated.

But Civet was busy studying the tops of Cloud Pass. "I thought I saw something too. Maybe we ought to fly above this pass."

But the rock walls had drawn closer, and Shimmer didn't dare turn around. "I'd have to rise higher, where the air's even thinner and colder."

"I already feel like my bones are turning to ice." Indigo had to fight to keep her teeth from chattering.

"I can't even feel my wings," Shimmer murmured.

"I'll take fur over scales anytime." I tumbled along overhead near the rock wall. "This just feels like a spring breeze." (That was a fib, of course.)

"Watch where you're going. You almost took my eye out with that bush." Civet tightened her legs around my waist and her arms around my neck.

"Strangle me," I gasped, "and you'll have to try walking on air." And when Civet had loosened her grip, I wondered, "What happened to your peaceful philosophy?"

"I want to be able to see the world," she grumbled, sounding more like her old self.

When something rattled against a rock just to our left, I searched all around. "What was that?"

Shimmer chuckled. "Just a rock. My, but you folks are jumpy as frogs."

I frowned at the mountain floor. There were only faint wisps of snow scudding before the wind. "There isn't supposed to be anybody living in the Desolate Mountains—except for the Smith and the Snail Woman."

Rocks clacked just ahead of us; and there, buried in the rocky wall itself, was an arrow, transparent as ice but unmistakable in shape.

"You can tell the hunters that." Shimmer winced as a wingtip scraped the canyon side. "And while you're at it, tell them that shooting arrows at someone isn't the best way to make friends."

"Where do they come from?" I wondered. "Something's very wrong."

Indigo had to punch Shimmer's shoulder with a fist in order to make her feel anything. "I say we find them and stomp them flat."

"This isn't a democracy," Shimmer informed her. "I don't fly by majority vote."

I descended about another ten meters, but there were only the ribbons of snow drifting along the caravan track and, farther on below, the thread of the river. "If I could find them, I'd teach those little sneaks some manners."

This time when we heard it, it was clearly a horn. And it was a lot closer. The notes bounced mockingly off the stony walls.

"Come out and fight," I shouted, and my challenge echoed up and down Cloud Pass. The next moment I had to give a little hop as an arrow ricocheted off a rock.

Whipping my tail back and forth, I watched as the arrow fell back toward the river. But there still wasn't any sign of who had shot it. I scratched under my cap in angry puzzlement. "It's like being hunted by ghosts."

"Who knows in the Desolate Mountains? Maybe it is ghosts." Civet was looking down intently. "The past has a way of being more real than the present."

Whoever our hunters were, they seemed content to keep pace beneath us—though every now and then they sounded a horn to remind us that they were still accompanying us.

"It's almost as if they were driving us," Civet frowned.

By the time we were halfway into Cloud Pass, its sides stretched for a kilometer above us, so we could see only a narrow streak of blue sky far overhead. Huge mounds of snow hid the face of the upper rock walls—looking for all the world like giant clouds that had perched on the cliff tops. Even so, scraggly fir trees fought to survive the cold as they clung precariously to the rocks.

"Quiet, everybody," Shimmer whispered. "Or we'll have an avalanche for sure."

I studied the snowdrifts above us. They were piled as high as castles. "Maybe we ought to fly above that for a while. Awk!"

I made the last sound when Civet tightened a forearm about my throat. "Shut up, you fool ape," she whispered. "It's already too late." She raised her other hand to point above us. At the top of either side of the pass, tiny figures in hooded white cloaks rose up where I would have sworn there was no one.

"Soldiers in camouflage," I gasped.

Indigo looked down at the caravan track. "There are more coming up behind us."

Suddenly the figures above us began flinging objects into the air. At a distance they looked like thin, milky strings. But as they fell, they spread outward quickly into large circular nets that seemed to change from one color of the rainbow to another: now red, then blue, then yellow.

"Quick." With a frantic beat of her wings, Shimmer shot forward. The more experienced Thorn knew enough to bend forward, but Indigo would have been blown off if she hadn't had such a tight grip on Thorn's waist. As it was, she nearly lost the disguised cauldron until she rested her head against his back.

At the same time I began to wheel through the air as a desperate Civet tried to cling to me. "I can't say I care much for their hospitality," I said. From the corner of one eye I could see a net. Some fifteen meters wide, the web was made all of glasslike fibers that reflected the light in different hues.

And then we had darted beyond it, and the net was descending behind us. But before I could congratulate Shimmer, I could see that we were flying underneath another net; and there were a dozen more nets falling in front and behind. In fact, Cloud Pass seemed full of giant spiderwebs.

Arching my tail around my waist, I plucked a handful of hairs from the tip. Then, spitting on the hairs, I threw them into the air. "Change," I whispered, and the hairs instantly turned into dozens of tiny monkeys. "Children, you have to gain me some time," I said as I dropped lower.

"Hold on," Shimmer told Thorn and Indigo, and banked to the side so that her left wing took most of the force of the net. Even so, the net's edge draped over her back, and some of the strands touched them.

Both the children gasped and Shimmer grunted and dipped dangerously. Though the net strands were only as thick as one of my fingers, they must have felt as heavy as a ship's cable. Shimmer shook her wing, but the net clung like hot tar and she began to plummet toward the icy river below.

CHAPTER ELEVEN

In a smart bit of flying, Shimmer whipped herself back to a regular flying position, flinging the edge of the net so that it clung to the rocks and spread outward like a giant spiderweb as she pulled back. Then her head darted forward and she snapped the net with a couple of quick nips of her fangs.

The snow men must have thrown their nets in waves, because there was another one dropping toward Shimmer, Thorn and Indigo. She went on completing the circle, so that her forelegs caught the edge of the net and threw it away.

"Hurry, children, hurry," I urged my little monkeys. "Find those troublemakers."

But a third net had draped itself over the dragon's head; and its glittering strands stretched down her neck and over her wings and back. Immediately the net drew in magically, so her wings were crushing her passengers against her back.

I will hand this to Shimmer: She knew how to handle herself in the air. Even with her wings bound, she managed to throw her weight so that she slammed down onto a ledge of snow belly first. There was a narrow overhang that sheltered the rear half of the ledge.

As I descended toward them, I began yanking handfuls of hairs from my tail and changing them into monkeys. Shimmer's jaws moved, but she couldn't speak—as if the magical tar had glued them shut.

By the time I landed on the ledge, my tail was pink and bald and there was a cloud of little monkeys around my head. "Cut the net," I ordered my children.

Up above, I could hear, the other group of monkeys were battling the snow men along the cliff's edge. As the noise grew louder, Civet jumped down from my back and tugged at the strands.

Shimmer began squeezing through a slit in the net that my little monkeys had made. She looked like a butterfly squeezing out of its cocoon. Angrily she spat out a black sticky lump. "I want to catch one of those snow men and ask them a few questions—like who made them." As she emerged, she opened her wings slightly so that the children could sit up.

Perhaps it was all the aerobatics, or perhaps the straps themselves were weak, but with a sharp snap the disguised cauldron fell from Thorn's back and bounced down Shimmer's side.

Immediately, Thorn threw himself off Shimmer and fell upon the cauldron before it could go over the ledge. "I got it," he cried.

Civet knelt beside him. "Are you all right?"

It took a few moments before the boy could get his breath back. He let go of the cauldron and sat up. Remembering the avalanche threat, he kept his voice low. "Just a few bruises." He couldn't help wincing as he stretched. "But I must have landed on them when I caught the cauldron."

"The net's vanishing," Indigo said, and we watched the severed strands of the net dissolve into thin tendrils of smoke.

Civet coughed and flapped a hand at one dark streamer. "It's magic."

"Very strong magic.". Shimmer's nostrils twitched. "But whose?"

"And what do they want?" I took out my staff

and expanded it. "This?" I nodded toward the cauldron cradled in Thorn's arms.

"I don't intend to stay around to find out." Shimmer frowned as Cloud Pass filled with the smoky outlines of more nets.

"Not when we're facing this much magic." I changed my staff to fighting size and twirled it in my hand.

"Better let me take the cauldron, butterfingers." Indigo was tying a knot in the broken strap. "We don't want you losing it again."

Resentfully, Thorn snatched up the cauldron. "It's my turn." And he strapped the cauldron over his back.

Suddenly the ledge began to vibrate under us. "Now what? More spells?" I peered up the face of the cliff and saw my children scampering back down toward me.

"Avalanche!" they were shouting, "avalanche!"

Outside in Cloud Pass, Thorn's little yelp about his turn was growing stronger and louder with each echo. Frightened, I remembered the huge hills of snow that had been poised on either side of the pass.

"Under the overhang," Civet said, and moved under that shelter.

"Why couldn't you keep quiet?" Indigo glared at Thorn as the rest of us joined Civet.

Already snow was trickling down on either side of the overhang to form mounds of snow on the ledge.

My paws a blur, I changed the little monkeys back into hairs and restored them to my tail.

Even as the rock itself began to shake with the vibrations, the snow spilled down from the overhang like a swaying gauze curtain that hid the opposite side of the pass. More snow piled up on the lip of the ledge and spread inward like a pool of milk.

Civet spread her legs for better balance and tried to find better footing on the snow-slick ledge. "We can't stop here."

"We'll have to risk flying." I had to shout to make myself heard above the roar of the falling snow. Shrinking my staff, I tucked it away and squatted down, motioning for Civet to climb on.

"Yes." Shimmer nodded to the children. "Get on."

However, either Indigo hadn't tied the knot tight enough or Thorn hadn't given her enough time to do it properly. As he waded through the snow toward Shimmer, the strap parted again and the gourd slid off his back. He tried to grab one of the straps as it fell, but he missed it; and then the gourd was bouncing and rolling merrily past him along the shaking, snow-covered ledge—as if it were doing a dance.

Fist-sized chunks of snow were dropping all around us, some of them landing on the ledge, bursting with loud explosions and showering the air with bursts of white flakes. It was like being in the middle of a battle.

Civet had been in the process of climbing onto my back, so when I lunged forward to help Thorn, she fell on her face in the snow. Thorn threw himself at the cauldron, but the straps flapped maddeningly just out of reach. As I waded in slow motion through the snow, I watched helplessly as the cauldron began to roll closer and closer to the edge. But with a desperate dive, he flung himself forward. Catching hold of one strap, he stopped it before it fell over.

Before we could celebrate, a boulder-sized hunk of snow fell on the boy. The weight must have been nearly as crushing as the cold was numbing, and Thorn lost his grip on the strap.

It was as if the cauldron were mocking us as it danced along the edge. Like a mole burrowing out of the ground, Thorn burst out of the snowbank. "I've got it," I told him as I tried to move through the now waist-high snow. But it was like moving through glue.

Scrambling on all fours, Thorn launched himself at the cauldron, which was now only a meter from the edge. Thorn stretched out his hands desperately, but a sudden rumbling in the mountains made the cauldron skip to the side, and Thorn's arms closed on empty air. His head twisting to watch the cauldron elude him once again, he went sliding through the snow toward the edge. He would have gone over except for Shimmer, who grabbed his collar.

In the meantime, though, Indigo had cut at an angle toward the lip of the ledge. Dropping to her knees, she tackled the cauldron; but the slippery snow made her slide along parallel to the edge.

Trees, snapped like twigs by the force of the avalanche, plummeted past the ledge, shooting like arrows toward the river below. More boulder-sized pieces of snow were thudding against the ledge, flinging white puffy clouds across the ledge. "Too late," I shouted. "We can't fly in that." I retreated toward the overhang again.

"We could be buried here." Shimmer was lifting Thorn up onto the cliff edge.

"Help!" Indigo yelped as she neared the edge.

"The cauldron." Evidently thinking Thorn was safe on the ledge, Shimmer reached out her long body to grab Indigo. But as she stretched, her wings brushed against Thorn. For one horrifying moment his arms flailed the air as he tried to gain his balance; and then he was falling toward the river, hidden by the white wall of avalanching snow.

As long as I live, I'll never forget that look on his face. It wasn't fear; it was the expression of someone who had lost everything—friends, loved ones, the entire world. It was terrible to think, too, that this moment would probably be his last memory.

"Thorn," Shimmer called even as her claws seized Indigo. "Thorn!" She stretched out her head past the ledge as if she were hoping to see and fly after him. However, in doing so, she had exposed her own head from underneath the overhang. A torrent of snow suddenly fell, knocking even her massive body over the edge. And with her went the screaming Indigo.

I tried to move back toward the rear of the ledge, but the snow was piling up and sweeping from one side to the other like a long shore current. The sheer weight of the newly fallen snow kept pushing more snow along—like a giant hand pushing sand.

"It's carrying us toward the edge." Civet struggled against the snow, but she was swept along relentlessly.

I tried to pull free, but the snow was now up to my chest. Inexorably, a cold, giant hand shoved both of us toward the pass. I looked up at the lip of the overhang and saw a sea of snow falling toward us. My last thought was that I had been right and Civet had been wrong. She wasn't going to die by fire after all.

And the next thing I knew, we were falling after the others. We fell encased in a world of white for what seemed forever.

CHAPTER TWELVE

It was dark. It was cold. It was wet. And someone was sobbing.

"Who's there? Where are we?" When I tried to get up, the world seemed to roll under me.

"Hey!" I heard Thorn say from near me.

I lay still, trying to use my other senses. I sniffed the air and smelled the fragrant scent of fir. "Are you all right?"

"Yes" came his muffled reply.

"But it sounded like you were crying." I felt underneath me. The texture was rough—like tree bark—and as my palms searched along, they felt some branches. We're in a tree, I thought.

"There's water gurgling all around us," Thorn said. "You must have heard that." However, there was still a catch in his voice.

The air was moving past my face. Or maybe we

were moving through the air. I thought a moment as we floated on through the darkness. "I guess a lot of trees got knocked down during the avalanche. I think we got snagged on one."

"Why is it dark?"

I tried to keep the fear from my own voice as I realized the reason. "The tree must have gotten swept along when the river went underground."

"Oh," he said in a small, frightened voice. "Do you have the cauldron?"

"I can't even find me," I said. However, when the sobbing began again, I tried to reassure him. "I'm sure that Shimmer is somewhere in the river. And if a dragon is in water, she'll be safe enough. And Civet lived in a river."

"What about Indigo?" he asked. "She had the cauldron."

And then I remembered what had happened on the ledge. "Yes, I saw."

"Without the cauldron, Shimmer's folk will die." And the sobbing began again. "Her poor, poor people."

"At this moment we have to worry about our own survival." It was hard on my nerves just floating in the dark without knowing what was ahead—or even around us. When I lifted my paw to try to feel the tunnel ceiling, the tree rolled slightly.

"But it's important to Shimmer," Thorn protested.

With more care I felt over my head, but there was nothing. The tunnel must be pretty big—for now. Even so, I decided that it was too risky to fly in the dark. "What Shimmer thinks isn't the only standard in this world."

"You don't understand," he said from the darkness. "You don't know what it was like living alone in that miserable village. And Knobby and all the others used to exercise their arms by hitting me. Even then, I'd just bite my lip so that I wouldn't cry out. Sometimes I'd even taste blood. But I'd never give them that satisfaction."

"It's not like you to complain," I sympathized.

With people who try to hold in all their troubles, it sometimes works a certain way. One crack in the jar and everything comes pouring out. "But," he went on, "there were times at night when I'd be lying on the hard floor in the kitchen, and I couldn't sleep though I had worked all day and was exhausted. There were too many bruises and welts to let me find a comfortable position. And there was no end in sight. I would be Thorn, the kitchen servant, forever—everyone's target and everyone's victim."

I was beginning to understand. "And then you met Shimmer."

"And I went with her," he agreed. "At first it was because anything—even deserts and monsters—seemed better than Knobby. But then I saw that underneath that tough hide of hers was a gentle person—though she would have growled and thumped her tail and denied everything."

"It takes a special person to love a dragon," I said. I didn't add that such things were beyond me.

"We've gone through some pretty hard times and saved each other's lives more than once." Suddenly his voice broke in a sob.

"It was an accident on the ledge," I tried to explain. "She thought you were safe, so she went to save Indigo next because she had the cauldron."

He sounded like just another lonely, lost child at the moment. "I keep telling myself that. But part of me keeps thinking that if neither of us had had the cauldron, she would have saved Indigo first."

I wanted to reach out and soothe him like I would any hurt child, but it was impossible in the dark. "She would have saved the nearest."

"No," he insisted. "Ever since Indigo joined us, I can't seem to do anything right, and she can't do anything wrong."

I tried to repeat Shimmer's reasons—though they hadn't sounded right to me even then. "She thought Indigo needed more self-confidence."

Thorn's voice became as bleak and harsh as stone grating on stone. "And on the ledge she saved her."

I suppose for Thorn it was like drowning at sea and finding a raft—only to have that raft fall apart. I tried to tell him that Shimmer still loved him as much as ever, that there was room in her heart for both of them—and all the other comforting things. But he was in such a panic that my words failed to reassure him.

"I'll show her," he swore fervently. "I'll prove to her that I'm just as clever as Indigo."

It's strange how some people can be so sharp about some things but so dense about others. "Now I've heard a few things in my time and seen a few things too; and I know that's wrong. It doesn't matter what others think of you—even if they're dragons. What's important is what *you* think of yourself."

But before he could answer, I heard branches snap off the tree and loud scraping sounds. "It sounds like it's a low bridge," I said. "Duck."

I pressed my own cheek against the tree trunk. Things began breaking overhead. Twigs and branches began raining onto my face, and I shut my eyes.

The tree began rolling to one side and then the other, and I felt a moment of panic when I felt rock begin to rasp by my fur and the tree itself sink lower into the water. And I began to wonder if this was going to be the end. Drowning in the dark was not the death I would have chosen. And as the rock began to scrape my face and the tree to buck under me, I got ready to die.

And suddenly we shot out into a huge underground cavern. There were crystal flowers all around the walls, and overhead were more crystals gleaming overhead with a soft, phosphorescent green light. And I realized I could see my paws. The fur was scraped off in spots, and there were cuts all over them.

We were definitely on a tree. I lifted myself up and looked carefully behind me. Thorn was farther down on the tree trunk, clinging with both hands to a large branch. He looked as badly banged up as I felt. Chunks of ice bobbed all around us.

And behind him was a narrow opening through which the river poured. Even as I watched, another tree shot out with a shower of breaking branches. On it was Indigo. Civet was on a third. She had lost her turban in the fall, and was not moving.

I looked ahead of me. There were more trees and saplings and ice accompanying us like a small fleet. And then I thought I saw something bobbing along.

"Is it Shimmer?" Thorn called anxiously. For all the wrong she had done him, he still forgave her.

"Well, it's either a moldy green log or a dragon." I glanced back at Thorn. "Not that there's much difference in their personalities." I rose from the tree, dripping water from my legs and robe, and somersaulted over the river until I was just above Shimmer. She seemed to be breathing all right; and I was so relieved to see her alive that I decided to have some fun.

Sitting down in midair, I slapped her on the head. "Hey, wake up."

"Oof." Shimmer sent up a spray of water straight into my face. "I'll get up in a moment, mother," she mumbled groggily. "Just let me sleep a little longer."

Stooping, I snatched up a big branch and bounced it off the top of her snout. "If I were a mother, I wouldn't have a baby as ugly as you."

The branch bounced off Shimmer, and she raised her head to blink her eyes indignantly at me. "I might have known it would take more than an avalanche to kill you."

I used my cap to wipe my face. "Are you trying to get a job as a fountain?"

Shimmer rubbed her injured snout. "It might be safer than this hero business."

"Thorn's back there," I whispered.

"Is he?" She waved a paw at him guiltily.

I drifted a little lower so Thorn wouldn't hear me. "An apology might be in order."

But I hadn't allowed for her confounded pride. "For what?" she asked in a loud, indignant voice. "I did what I had to do back on the ledge." And she called back to Thorn before I could stop her, "You understand, don't you, boy?"

If I'd had my staff handy, I would have clubbed her. As it was, I could only put a finger to my lips. "Hush."

But Shimmer could be as stubborn as she was proud. "Thorn, you understand."

And it was a measure of how much Thorn loved the dragon that he said meekly, "Yes."

Shimmer rolled a smug eye toward me. "So, you furry busybody, I'll thank you to keep your snout out of my affairs."

"Hey," Indigo called from her tree. "There's the cauldron."

She pointed at the gourd's round sides bobbing along in the river. "Well, aren't you the clever girl," Shimmer praised her.

Remembering our recent conversation, I glanced back to see how poor Thorn took it. But he was hiding his feelings as he usually did. Even so, I was sure it hurt him inside.

Intending to fly, Shimmer spread out her leathery wings; but I had already stood up in midair and waved my wet cap. "No, no, it's Monkey to the rescue as usual." With a bow, I set my dripping cap on my head.

Kicking, Shimmer shot underneath me through the water, wending her way among the other floating trees. "Take your bows after you save the cauldron, you idiot."

With a laugh, I began somersaulting through the air. "Where is all that famous dragon tact and wit I've heard about?"

Shimmer lifted her head out of the water to talk more easily. "They never had to deal with you."

Flying at my fastest, I couldn't keep up with a dragon swimming. "Slowpoke," she called, raising a saillike wing in triumph. "The old pot's fine. There's just some water that leaked in through the crack." Holding the gourd carefully to her, she began to swim back.

"Aaa-rooo-o-o-o-o-o." A dog's howl echoed and reechoed from the cavern's walls.

"Hurry," Thorn urged.

I spun in the air and for the first time saw the dark bulk of the island looming to our right. I had been so busy with the others and the cauldron that I hadn't noticed it before. It was about a hundred meters long with the strangest brush fringing its sides, for it glowed a soft violet color. And behind it were the oddest trees, some as much as twenty meters high with wide umbrella tops. The trunks were also the strangest colors—some even with yellow spots on red trunks. And beyond them was the funniest sort of hill—oval shaped like an egg and just as white and smooth.

As we drew even with the island, the brush began to shake with soft whispering sounds. Somersaulting high over the floating trees, I joined Thorn again and changed my staff to weapon size.

Suddenly, with an odd squishing sound, a giant dog shoved its way through the brush and along the beach. As huge as a pony, it was covered with white fur; and its red eyes seemed to glow like two coals. Barking, it kept pace with us as we floated by the island. And its barks sounded like drumbeats inside the cavern. It leaped upon a huge boulder.

"Excitable type, isn't it?" I observed.

Shimmer swam up to Indigo's tree and handed the cauldron to her. "Quit making jokes and start looking for a way to get out of here," she snapped.

"I should've known." I sighed. "All that soaking wouldn't soften a dragon."

The strange trees were moving swiftly by then, and the end of the island slid by. Thorn tried to say something, but I couldn't hear him for the noise. The cavern walls pinched in at this point, and some trick of the acoustics had hidden the sound up until now. But I knew what it was like to be inside a tiger's throat when it let out a roar.

Twisting around, I looked ahead of us and saw a tree's roots suddenly tilt upward. "There's a waterfall ahead," I said, but I could barely hear myself, let alone make anyone around me hear me.

However, the others had realized the truth at the same time. Shimmer was writhing and splashing, trying to keep the strong current from dragging Indigo's tree over. I rose in the air and seized hold of the roots of our tree while Thorn tried to help by paddling with his hands.

But as we struggled in the water, the tree with the unconscious Civet shot past. I looked helplessly from our tree to hers. I couldn't hold both. Neither could Shimmer.

The dog barked sharply again, as if it wanted my attention. I saw the boulder upon which it stood. Quickly I set one loop of my staff over the thickest of the tree roots. "Change," I shouted, and the iron rod grew and grew, stretching itself as thin as a string. When the dog saw what I was trying to do, it leaped down from the boulder so I could fit the other end over the point of the rock.

Well, that's all easier said than done. My staff was now some twenty meters long, and I was busy with the tree. However, after only a couple of tries I managed to secure the staff.

Then, letting go of the tree, I watched cautiously—ready to intervene if necessary. The tree gave a jerk but stopped. Both the tree roots and the staff were strong enough. Reassured, I cartwheeled quickly through the air to help Civet.

I had just stopped Civet's tree when Thorn shouted, "No, leave the staff where it is." I looked up to see that the giant white dog had removed the golden loop from the rock and was beginning to back up, moving from the beach toward the strange forest. As it disappeared into the bushes, Thorn's tree began gliding smoothly against the river currents toward the island.

"Let go of that staff," I yelled at the dog.

I could barely hear Indigo's shout as Thorn sped past her. "Take the staff off your tree."

Picking up the unconscious Civet, I slung her over my shoulder and began to leap back toward Thorn. I figured that I could rest her on Thorn's tree while I held it away from the falls.

My staff was slithering through the bushes so fast that they kept giving off bursts of purple light. And Thorn's tree was moving toward the island so fast that the water foamed white in front of it. Reaching his hands up, he began to try to shove the golden loop from the roots. "It's stuck," he said, and looked back at Shimmer.

Shimmer was holding on to Indigo's tree. "I can't let go of Indigo," she said.

Thorn's face fell as if it were the ledge all over again. And then Indigo called to him. "Cut the roots, then."

That was the last straw as far as Thorn was concerned. "Will you quit bossing me around? I'm not your servant." And he went on trying to free the loop from the wood.

But the next moment the log had thumped against the island. With another yank at my staff, the dog jerked the tree into the air so that it landed on the beach. Satisfied, the dog dropped my staff.

Thorn slid off on one side, glancing anxiously back at the woods for the dog while he tried to free my staff from the tree roots.

Carrying Civet, I dropped down on the beach beside him. Quickly picking up the end of my staff, I shouted, "Change." But instead of shrinking to weapon size, it remained stretched out.

Deciding to puzzle it out later, I set the staff down. "Get behind me," I said to Thorn, and got ready with my fists to meet our host.

CHAPTER THIRTEEN

Shimmer, with Indigo on her back, swam onto shore a moment later. "Can you see that dog?"

"No." Now that Shimmer was here, I thought it was safe to investigate my staff. But try as I would, I couldn't shrink it down. "My staff won't shrink."

"Getting forgetful?" she asked.

"Of course not." I glanced at the dragon and noticed that she was looking carefully away from Thorn—as if her conscience were bothering her about what she had done back on the ledge or just now near the waterfall.

As Indigo climbed off, she pointed at the sparkling lights in the ceiling. "Those look like stars."

"It must be minerals." Shimmer prowled past me to feel one of the bushes. "And these aren't real bushes at all. They're lichen."

Still keeping hold of my staff, I shook myself like

a wet dog, trying to get the water from my fur. "This isn't exactly the spot I would pick for a vacation."

Thorn was helping the groggy Civet to sit up. "How do you think the dog got here?"

"Who knows?" I set my useless staff down again as the bushes began to shake. "Now hush."

The next moment the bushes parted. The strange, giant dog stood there, its red eyes regarding us silently. In its jaws it held a sack, which it deposited on the sand. Then it withdrew to the bushes again, where it watched us.

Indigo got up. "Maybe it brought us something to eat."

"I'm nobody's pet," Shimmer grumbled.

"Nice doggy," Indigo said as she trudged up the beach toward the sack. "Nice doggy," she kept murmuring.

The dog didn't stir as Indigo picked up the sack and retreated back to us. "It smells like fish," she said, sniffing.

We all caught a whiff of fish. "It smells smoked," I added.

We crowded around as Indigo opened the sack and took out a hammer, crudely made from a stone tied to a stick. "Somehow I don't think I'll be making a midnight snack out of this."

Impatiently, Indigo overturned the sack and emptied out its contents and began arranging them methodically. "Needles in assorted sizes. Spools of thread and yarn and rawhide."

I examined a long needle fashioned from some big fish bone. "Some of it homemade, too."

Shimmer picked up a jar. "And the rest was probably salvaged from the river." She broke the clay seal on the lid. "What's this?"

I waved a hand in front of my nostrils. "Phew, it smells like dead fish."

Shimmer tested it with a claw and then wiped it on the sack. "It's glue."

We went through the rest of the contents quickly. There was a stone axe, an adze and other tools as well. "It's a tool kit," Indigo said in disappointment.

"There's someone else." Thorn pointed.

I looked up to see the bushes rustling a few meters away from the watchful dog. "It seems like the dog isn't the only one here."

But when I started forward, the white dog sprang out, red eyes gleaming like coals; and its upper lip drew back in a snarl.

"Excuse me," I said, halting.

The white dog only let out a deep growl in unmistakable warning.

"Spare the rod and spoil the dog." I got ready to give the dog one of my double kicks.

Shimmer caught hold of my tail. "Don't you think that it's enough to have two armies after us? Do we have to make more enemies?"

I freed my tail. "I suppose you have a point."

But the next moment the dog whirled around and disappeared into the forest. Cautiously, I approached the other spot and saw a huge smoked trout.

"It must have been a waiter." I stared at the dirt and muttered, "Well, well, but I didn't see any tracks." Along the surface were smooth marks, as if someone had dragged a heavy sack to cover his or her tracks. "I've heard of shy, but this is going too far."

Indigo joined me. "Food." It took both her hands to lift the trout.

"It's probably poisoned," Civet said from behind us.

Indigo hunkered down. "If it wanted to kill us, it could have let us drown. At any rate, I'm hungry enough to eat a log." Tearing at the side, she picked up a piece and stuffed it into her mouth. With a teasing smile on her face she chewed while we all watched her intently. Now that Indigo was eating, my own stomach began to grumble. And I wasn't the only one.

"You'd better have some before I eat it all up." Indigo stretched out a sandy hand, offering me a piece. Without bothering to clean it off, I took it. The next moment the trout had disappeared under a flurry of hands and paws.

When we had reduced the fish to a skeleton, Shimmer stretched and yawned. "I don't think this place will be making any lists as holiday resort despite all the hospitality. Shall we go?"

Thorn reached for the cauldron, but Indigo beat him to it. I didn't say anything about their little games as they jockeyed for Shimmer's favor. Both of them had led hard, lonely lives. I just wished they had been able to share Shimmer more.

Before Thorn could argue, Indigo had scurried up on top of Shimmer. From her high perch she strapped on the cauldron. Retreating sullenly, Thorn picked up the sack of tools.

"Don't weigh us down with that trash." Shimmer frowned.

Thorn clung stubbornly to the sack. "But they might come in useful."

"Shimmer's not a ferry barge," Indigo said.

"That's right," Shimmer was quick to agree.

Remembering our conversation in the dark, I wanted to head off trouble. "I'll take Thorn and the sack," I said.

"It's your back," Shimmer mumbled, and motioned for Civet to climb up behind Indigo.

Once Thorn had mounted me, I picked up my long staff. "I feel a little breeze, so there must be some opening in the ceiling. Keep a sharp lookout." Slowly I began to slide my hands along the shaft so I could take it up with me, intending to find out what was wrong with it later.

However, as I was trying to balance it, the golden loop at one end seemed to hit something. I peered behind me, but all I saw was empty air over the river. "That's funny." I poked again and once more felt the loop strike an unseen obstruction. "There's some kind of barrier around the island."

By now Shimmer had already risen with a flap of her wings. "This is no time for clowning," she scolded.

I poked at the water. "It's underneath the surface of the river too."

Shimmer rose slowly, testing the air above the

island until her tail struck an invisible ceiling. "There's magic here, but it has an odd smell."

"Do you think it's the old magic?" I asked.

Shimmer landed on the beach, and her passengers slid back onto the sand. "We rose. Maybe we can swim under whatever magical barrier is there."

I gave a little unhappy shiver when I looked at the water. Chunks of ice were still floating by on the cold surface. But Civet tucked up her skirt around her legs. "It's my turn." And she waddled down to the water. She tested it with her foot and gave a shudder. "But it's colder than a landlord's heart."

Thorn quietly began to gather firewood into a heap. "Maybe we'd better get a fire going."

"Have faith," Civet said. Crouching, she took a deep breath and crawled into the water. We could see her silhouette just beneath the surface as she kicked and shoved, but she couldn't move a centimeter.

Gasping, she raised her head out of the water. "It's no use. There's something holding me here." The moment she stopped struggling, it was as if a giant invisible hand carried her back toward shore.

Setting my staff down again, I squatted down over

a piece of driftwood. "Magic may not work on this island. That may be what's wrong with my staff." I made a sign with my fingers and muttered a spell. When nothing happened, I repeated myself.

When I failed a second time, Shimmer laughed. "Ha! Better let me try." But she had no more success than I had.

"No magic," Shimmer sniffed. "That's barbaric. That means we have to be like—"

"Humans," Thorn said, taking his flint and steel out of his pouch.

"No offense meant," Shimmer said hastily.

Shivering with the cold and wet, Civet glanced sideways at Shimmer. "How does it feel to lose your magic?"

"Not very good," I admitted. In fact, I felt as if I had lost an arm or a leg. And from Shimmer's stunned expression, I knew she felt the same way.

No one said anything while Thorn got the fire going. Fortunately there was plenty of wood. I watched the smoke drift upward. "Look. I bet there's a crack across there." I pointed across the water, where the smoke wriggled like a snake. "If there wasn't an opening up there, the smoke would just hover in the middle of the cave."

Civet watched the steam rise from her clothes.

"The question is how to get there. You can get onto this island, but you can't get off. I mean, it's a prison. You can catch fish from the water and you can get driftwood from the beach."

Shimmer sighed. "Whoever came up with this island had an exquisite sense of humor."

I thought again of the erased tracks. "You don't go to that sort of trouble just to build a kind of kennel." I looked back at the island. "Just who is imprisoned here?"

CHAPTER FOURTEEN

Thorn was just as eager to prove himself as he had confessed to me when we had been floating on the tree. And all our failures just made him more determined than ever to get us off the island.

While everyone else slumped on the beach, Thorn picked up the sack. It was made from the hide of some animal—perhaps some mountain goat washed down from outside. He took out the jar of glue and poured a drop onto a piece of wood. Then he dipped his hand into the surf and dribbled water onto the glue. "It's waterproof," he said.

He stared at the sack for a moment and then excitedly began taking the items one by one and laying them out on the sand. "We were wrong. It's not just a tool kit. What we have here is your basic boat-building kit."

I squatted down beside him and examined the adze. The edge looked used. "Either we're not wanted or our host wants us to build a boat for him or her."

Indigo joined us. "Or to show him or her how to do it." And we all glanced behind us at the bushes, but there was no sign of the white dog.

Shimmer rubbed the back of her long neck. "Funny, I can't see anyone, but I've got this strange feeling we're being watched."

Civet picked up the axe, holding it near the head. "That's not our concern." And pivoting on her heel, she strode up the beach.

Shimmer roused. "And just where do you think you're going?"

Civet stared her down coolly. "To do something I never thought I'd be doing again."

Mushrooms grew on tall, thin green stalks among the lichen bushes; and with her axe she began to cut them. "These are just like reeds."

"So?" Indigo looked up from the jar of glue she had been examining.

"So"—Civet brought an armload of cut mushrooms and dumped them down near the tools—"it means I haven't lost the knack after all these centuries."

"For what?" I flicked some mushroom tops from my lap. "Landscaping?"

Civet deftly used the large axehead to trim the tops from the mushrooms. She smiled to herself slightly. "Building a reed boat. My people used to make them all the time." She began to slice one stalk into long, fine strips.

I tried to picture it in my head but couldn't. "How d'you keep the water out?"

"You don't." Civet began to twist the stalks into a tight bundle. "But the water goes in as fast as it goes out, so the boat floats right along."

We all gathered around as she used some of the strips to tie the bundles fast. "A boat would be made up of bunches of reeds," she explained, "but this will do for a test."

However, when Civet set her little toy upon the water, it stayed put as if it were glued to the surface. "Go on," she said angrily, and tried to shove it.

But the little boat snapped, and she fell into the water. When Civet had been fished from the river, Indigo pulled at her lip. "Maybe the magic affects boats. But what about a sack of air?"

"Yes, that might just get around the spell." Shimmer nodded her head.

With the needles and some strips of leather from the sack, we sewed it up, then sealed it with glue except for one opening.

"Here." Shimmer motioned for me to take the sack. "You've got all the hot air. You inflate it."

With a bow and a flourish of my arm, I indicated that she should take it. "I'm not the one who's always boasting about her pedigree."

"Pet dogs have pedigrees," Shimmer corrected me icily. "Dragons have lineages. And I only mention my ancestors because they provide such an uplifting example for the young." The dragon flicked her claw back and forth between Thorn and Indigo.

Civet had spread her hair out to dry faster. "In the meantime, you're both wasting your wind in this silly argument."

"Well, I vote for Monkey," Indigo said.

"With Shimmer as a backup," Civet added.

Recognizing a summons to greatness, I jumped to my feet and gave a mock bow. "Thank you for this great honor. It's not every day that a dragon will acknowledge her inferiority to a monkey."

"I never did any such thing," Shimmer growled.

"Then here." I tried to present the sack to her.

But for once the overgrown lizard figured out what

I was up to. "Oh, no." Shimmer wagged her paw. "After you. When it comes to being a windbag, I'm willing to concede."

I arched an eyebrow at Thorn. "Mark this day on a monument." And taking a deep breath, I set the opening of the sack to my lips and began to blow. My cheeks puffed out until they ached and I could feel my eyeballs bulging. And slowly the sack began to swell out between my paws.

Shimmer began to clap her paws together. "I do believe the little fur bag has found a vocation."

When the sack was inflated and sealed with glue, we let it dry. Unfortunately, despite all our elaborate preparations, the sack refused to budge once we set it on the water. We wouldn't be able to float off the island either.

I have to admit that even I was beginning to feel discouraged. Shimmer's head, with her long neck, sagged miserably. Only Civet, with her new resolve, seemed willing to try to make the best of it. "Well, it's not as if we were trapped in some desert. The place is pretty enough. And it's not as if we're going to starve. There's always fish to catch."

"Spare us the philosophy," Indigo snapped.

"Every day that we're alive is a victory," Civet

insisted. "So let's have lunch. How about trying to surf fish?"

However, our failures only seemed to make Thorn think twice as hard. Suddenly he sprang to his feet. "It's the spell. It's not supposed to work like a wall. It's a filter, because obviously our host can catch fish. Now whoever cast the spell thought of the obvious things like swimming and boating—and some of the less obvious things like floating on a sack. But whoever did it couldn't think of everything."

Thorn's optimism was infectious. Shimmer sprang up. "Let's search the island."

"But as a group," I said, rising to my feet. "I'll take the lead. Indigo, Thorn and Civet should be in the middle. Shimmer can bring up the rear."

Shimmer frowned. "A dragon should be in the vanguard."

"Where her big behind will block everyone else's view." I waved her to the rear. "Don't worry. I have a feeling that you'll have plenty of chances to prove your bravery before we get off this island."

We found a wide, spacious trail, and I squatted down to study the mud. "More dog tracks." I motioned to the funny swept marks. "It looks as if our host has been here too and erased his tracks."

Leaving my staff regretfully on the beach, I started on the trail. The lichen bushes gave way to those strange trees with thick red trunks dotted with yellow spots. High overhead their tops shut out the shining little lights of the ceiling. Putting a hand against the trunk, I showed the others how spongy it was. "I think these are giant mushrooms."

All along the trail mosses grew in globe shapes with weird ridges that reminded me of giant brains—except these were all different colors and glowed with a pale, ghostly light. Other places there were patches of lichen that grew in strange shapes— some were in the form of vases, others fans of delicate lace. Some grew taller than me. Others rose flowerlike with tall, thin, purple stems that spread out in clusters of green, berrylike tops.

"Wait," Civet called. And when I turned, I saw Civet bending over curiously. "This looks like . . . No, it couldn't be. The book said it had disappeared a long time ago." She touched a fanlike lichen, and it curled away from her palm. "But it is." When she closed her hand around a lacy section, the whole fan convulsed.

Shimmer stopped her suspiciously. "It isn't poison, is it?"

Civet let go indignantly. "It's good for healing wounds."

I gazed at a cluster of bright, purple mushrooms. "I recognize these from above. But there are other mushrooms here that I've never seen before."

Civet rubbed her arm where Shimmer had grabbed her. "Probably because they vanished from outside. This island has whatever spores washed down the river."

"How charming—a fungus museum." Shimmer shoved the others forward impatiently. "Perhaps next we'll see a toadstool in the shape of my uncle Sambar."

As we followed the track, I couldn't help looking all around the strange forest. I had no idea that mushrooms and toadstools could come in so many shapes and sizes. There were as many bright colors as a flower garden. In fact, the whole place would have been beautiful except for a curious musty, rotting smell.

Suddenly a lion's head popped out of a patch of blue, flower-shaped mushrooms.

"Watch out." I shoved Indigo back and raised my fists in front of me.

"That's a stone lion," Indigo said from behind me.

Squinting, I leaned forward and saw that what I had thought was fur was really yellow lichen covering it. And on the other side of the path I saw a second lion. I lowered my fists. "I'm no art expert, but even I can see that they're different styles."

Indigo peered around me. "And why are their muzzles so worn? There's no rain to weather them."

"Perhaps they got worn from being washed down the river," Civet said from behind us.

Encouraged, I pushed on. "Then it's more than spores that wound up on this island. We just may find something that will take us away from here."

A grove of treelike toadstools had screened the white dome from sight. But we saw the egg-shaped building now. At its highest, I would have said, it rose some ten meters.

Civet studied the strange structure. "Is this the egg that the mountain is named after?"

Shimmer shrugged. "Who knows? Anyone who could have told us is long since dust."

The dirt courtyard in front of the dome was filled with the worn, waterstained flotsam that had been washed down the river, including almost a hundred small jars. Shimmer, who had seen a few things in the centuries she had lived, examined the piles of junk. "It really is like a museum—a little bit of every era."

I examined a blood-red bowl with cordlike impressions in the sides. "Or an antique shop run by a pack rat."

"Hello," Indigo called.

I whirled around to see the girl on her hands and knees before an opening that was only a meter high and quite wide. A soft, eerie glow spilled from within. When there wasn't any answer, she looked over her shoulder at the rest of us. "The owner must be pretty short."

Crowding around, we peered inside. The building was lit by glowing tapestries of lichen that hung down from the ceiling—at least they had the appearance of tapestries, with blockish figures of men and women.

Beneath the tapestries was a hodgepodge of furniture of various styles, all of it water damaged to some degree. There was even a huge, cylindrical pottery lamp, as tall as Shimmer—perhaps intended for some mansion. A lonely blue flame rose from its spout.

Indigo pointed toward a row of five couches, each of them made from antique, water-stained cushions, pillows and sacks stuffed with something—probably more lichen. Four of them were normal sized, and one of them was long enough even for a dragon. On each were sheets of lichen and what were smaller pillows of moss. "We've been given food and we've been given shelter."

"Our host expects us to be here quite a while," Civet said.

"Not if I can help it," I said grimly. "Come on. Let's start looking."

Creeping through the doorway, I tapped the tapestries and poked underneath and around the furniture. "Everything seems fine—just a little musty smelling."

As soon as she heard that it was safe, Indigo slid in and headed straight over toward a black teak mirror box that she had spotted. It was the kind that people used when they were traveling. "My hair's in a mess," she said, fussing with her blue spikes of hair. Quickly the girl lifted the box lid and set it in place at an angle so she could use the mirror that was usually on the inside of the lid. "That's funny. There's no mirror inside." She examined the box. "But otherwise there isn't even a chip to the lacquer."

Civet pointed toward another box. "There's one over there."

However, when Indigo lifted the lid, it also was missing its mirror—though it was in good shape otherwise. Quickly I inspected the other furnishings, trying to find something shiny—not so much to please Indigo as to satisfy my own curiosity. The furnishings were whatever had washed up on the beach, and they ranged from the expensive to the very ordinary—depending on what had probably fallen from some caravan pack into the river.

But there wasn't anything that would show a reflection.

"Well, well, well, well," I muttered to myself. "So our host is a shy one."

"Come on," Thorn called impatiently. "I thought I saw an old wok out in the courtyard."

Back in the courtyard we found the wok. It was big enough for each of us to go one at a time. "Funny that there are rust stains on it, though," I said.

Thorn tipped it on its side and rolled it near the head of the trail. "They're probably souvenirs from floating in the river. Try to find something else. Think of anything that has the proper shape to float. We're not trying to win a contest for the most beautiful boat—anything that's like a raft or a boat."

So we scattered through the courtyard, pawing through the piles of junk. And when we each had an armload of possibilities, we followed Thorn as he rolled the wok back to the beach.

Unfortunately, none of them worked.

Discouraged, we sat down among the heaps of junk that now littered the beach. Shimmer hammered the wok. "We should have realized—the junk was in the courtyard because our host has already tried it."

Civet lay down on the sack of air. "And then couldn't get rid of it." I shook my head. "Whoever put the spell on this island really did think of everything."

Shimmer sat glumly on her haunches. "Our host didn't collect all this trash overnight. He must have been here for years. In that time, he must have tried everything."

I doffed my cap and waved it in acknowledgment to those unknown magicians who had created this island prison. "Now *that*," I admitted, "is some spell."

"So," Indigo said, slumping, "we're trapped here forever."

CHAPTER FIFTEEN

It was silent on the beach. And then Thorn slowly rose and went over to Shimmer. "You're not giving up already? You and I have been in tight places before."

"But nothing like this." A discouraged Shimmer pointed at the invisible barrier.

I motioned for Thorn to sit down again. "You're a regular little bulldog, aren't you? Sink your teeth into the notion of helping us escape and you won't let go. At least take a rest."

Thorn planted his fists on his hips. "We've tried everything probable. That only leaves the improbable."

Shimmer's forehead knitted together in puzzlement. "Such as?"

Licking his lips, Thorn began to tick off the items on his fingers. "Well, there's fire and water if we could change ourselves into either form. But our magic doesn't work here."

"So now what?" Indigo demanded.

Thorn plopped back down on the sand. "So I have to think some more." Idly he picked up a pebble and began to throw it from hand to hand.

"It's all very well to make nice speeches, but the truth is a different matter." Indigo yawned.

Angrily Thorn twisted around and whipped the pebble up above his shoulder. For a moment I thought Thorn was angry enough to throw the pebble at her.

"You're making a big mistake," Indigo warned him quietly.

"That's enough of that." Shimmer extended one large paw as a wall between them.

Frustrated, Thorn twisted around to face the river again and whipped the pebble away from him. It was round and flat, so it skipped one, two, three hops before it sank.

Indigo leaned forward as if to say something nasty again, but she paused when she saw Thorn's face. "Thorn, are you all right?"

However, Thorn simply ignored her. He sat there, staring at the spot where the pebble had sunk.

"Thorn?" Shimmer wondered.

Suddenly, Thorn bent and began searching through the pebbles in the sand until he had another half dozen round, flat pebbles. Then, one by one, he skipped them out over the river.

Afraid that the boy had finally lost his senses, I got up. "Are you all right, Thorn?"

With all the solemnity of a judge, Thorn rose. Then, raising one hand over his head, he threw himself into an almost professional cartwheel. Unfortunately he landed right on top of Indigo.

As he lay there laughing, she crawled out from underneath him. With a nervous glance at the still laughing boy, she whispered, "He's cracked."

Thorn raised himself on one elbow. "On the contrary, I've never been better."

Indigo slid backward through the sand away from him. "You ought to go lie down."

Thorn seized handfuls of sand and waved them at us. "Don't you see? Whoever built this prison had to consider one thing: Sand and dirt and rocks would be washed down that river night and day, year after year, century after century. And it would all pile up here on this island, so it would spread wider and wider until it silted up the river. And wouldn't that be a mess? Maybe the cave would fill with water until the mountain broke. And maybe even the spell would be broken."

I gathered a pawful of sand and looked at it. "So rocks can wash away, and so can sand and dirt."

Shimmer pondered the beach and then shook her head. "Unfortunately, we can't transform ourselves into stones or sand either." Thorn threw the sand over his head. "But we don't have to. If sand and dirt can leave, I bet clay could."

Shimmer knitted her forehead in puzzlement. "But we can't change ourselves into clay either."

Thorn spread out his arms as he spun around. "What about *fired* clay? What about a pot? Pots are just fired clay."

"That big lamp back at the house." I sprang up. "We were so busy looking for boats and rafts, we missed the obvious."

Shimmer rose and did a gleeful little stomp of her own, beaming at Thorn. "Thorn, I think you've done it this time."

But before Thorn could bask in the glory of the moment, we heard an urgent howl from the bushes. Suddenly there came a crashing sound, and through the lichen we could see a huge white shape galloping back toward the house.

I looked regretfully at my useless staff. I felt unarmed without it. "Come on. We've got to beat that dog to the lamp."

"I can't fly off the island, but I can fly underneath the barrier." Spreading her wings, Shimmer leaped into the air. I tried to follow her and fell face first in the sand. Since Shimmer depended on her own muscles to fly, the ban on magical spells didn't affect her; but it did me.

Without even waiting to brush the sand from my fur, I had bounced to my feet and was off and running. There was very little on hoof, paw, or foot that could keep up with me in a race; and the next moment I had overtaken Indigo, Thorn, and Civet.

"Coming through," I shouted, and ran around them on the wide trail.

The only one I couldn't catch was Shimmer, who shot ahead like a lean, green arrow and disappeared in the courtyard ahead of me. As I thumped along the path, I heard barking and snarling from the strange house.

"I've got him," Shimmer shouted to me. "Ow."

I darted into the courtyard, where Shimmer was circling round and round like a top, dragging the dog along like a toy as he held on to her tail. There were skid marks all around as the dog tried to dig its paws in and halt the dragon.

I leaned against the gate to enjoy the spectacle. "If I didn't know any better, I'd say that you don't have the dog. The dog has you."

"Ow, ow, ow." Shimmer grimaced. The dog must have some set of fangs to bite through Shimmer's hide. "Get rid of this mutt."

But I simply groomed the fur on my face "Say please."

"I'd rather die, you little fur bag."

I buffed my nails on my robe. "Suit yourself, but I've heard of a snake that can swallow a cow that's twice its size. It just takes a while."

In vain Shimmer tried to kick at the dog with her hindpaws. Then she tried swinging her tail back and forth, but the dog stuck to her like glue, so all Shimmer achieved was to scatter the junk around the courtyard.

She finally halted. "Please," she panted.

However, it wasn't often that I got to take a dragon down a peg. I put a paw behind my ear. "Pardon?"

"PLEASE!" Shimmer yelled at me.

I toyed with the notion of having her say "Please with honey on top"; but the murderous expression on her face made me think better of it. "Everything happens for someone who's polite." Finding a bamboo pole in the trash, I gently rapped the dog on its noggin, and it fell over unconscious.

By that time the others had reached the courtyard. As Shimmer carefully extricated her tail from the dog's jaws, she glared at me. "Next time you can be the decoy."

Staying carefully out of range, I curled my own tail up in the air. "With this skimpy tail?"

Indigo went right away to Shimmer and asked solicitously, "Is it bleeding?"

I found a long piece of rope. "I'd be more worried about that poor dog's teeth."

But Thorn, remembering what Civet had said, broke off a bit of one of the fanlike lichens that grew near one of the stone lions. It wriggled in his hand like worms. "What do we do?" he asked Civet.

"Wait a moment," Shimmer said cautiously.

"If it was poisonous, it would have killed Thorn already." And Civet rubbed her palms together. "Bruise it and then press it against the wounds."

"Give me some," Indigo said. She seemed genuinely worried about Shimmer.

But by now Thorn was annoyed enough with her to hold on to the medicine. "I can do it."

"My grandfather's whiskers," Shimmer snapped. "It'll go faster if you *both* cooperate."

Reluctantly, Thorn had to admit to the reasonableness of Shimmer's suggestion and handed some over to his rival. But when he bent to apply it, Thorn observed, "The dog didn't break through the skin. There are just a lot of little dents there."

"Just in case, though." And Indigo insisted on putting the lichen on anyway, so of course Thorn also put some on.

In the meantime I had lashed the white dog's legs together with the rope. Civet, who had stood over me and supervised, advised, "Tighter."

However, I ignored her. "It's enough to keep it from giving us any more trouble. But it should be able to work out of its bonds after we're gone."

"The dog isn't our problem. Escaping is," she insisted.

I finished tying one last knot. "This poor beast might have been guilty of nothing more than being loyal to our host. In any event, it's done us no harm."

"That's a matter of opinion." Shimmer sniffed indignantly.

"But," Thorn observed, "what if the dog and our host haven't done any wrong? Maybe they're innocent and were trapped here by some bad wizard."

"Maybe they are and maybe they aren't. But I'm not taking any chances. They can stay here till the next big pot comes down. Come on. Let's get the lamp," I said, and started for the house.

But Shimmer held back, searching among the fungus surrounding the track. "I would have sworn that I saw something drop off the dog's back."

"You got excited in the battle." I crawled into the house.

The big lamp was standing right where we had left it, but the flame was out. I measured it with my arms. "If we could cut it lengthwise, we could use it like a canoe."

I had one of the children open a chest, which proved to be empty. Then I carefully poured the lamp's oil into the chest. "No sense of making a mess for our host."

When the lamp was empty, we tipped it over on its side and slid it top first through the low, wide doorway and out into the courtyard. Civet swept up a long length of rope and shook it at me. "I told you to tie this tighter. The dog got away."

I frowned and hunted around the bushes. "It couldn't have gotten loose this soon."

"So what? We have the lamp now." Indigo threw herself at the lamp, and it began to rumble forward. "And there's nothing else large enough to let it get away."

I think the confinement and the frustrations had

finally taken their toll on Civet's philosophy. "You're all idiots." Civet flung the now useless rope to the side.

"You can stay on the island if you like," Shimmer snapped.

Thorn put a hand on Civet's arm. "Don't say anything that you'll regret later."

Civet swallowed hard. And then, with a strange, fierce look, she seized the boy's hand and squeezed it as if she could press her warning directly into his flesh. "More and more I think that I saw visions and not nightmares. If so, don't listen to these jabbering fools. The world will depend upon you and you alone."

Uncomfortable, Thorn pulled his hand free with some difficulty. "Let's hope this poor world never gets into such a mess that it has to depend upon me." And bending over, he joined Indigo by the lamp.

"Pushing it will take forever," I said, and leaped up on top of the lamp's side. "My way is quicker."

"Careful," Shimmer warned.

I only tipped my cap forward. "I'd like to see the dragon nimble enough to do this." And with quick slaps of my feet, I began rolling the lamp down the wide track.

Shimmer bowled over both Indigo and Thorn as she rushed after me. "Quit showing off. You could break it." And raising a paw, she grabbed hold of the lamp's top.

The trouble was that the lamp stopped, but I didn't. I went flying head over heels, burrowing headfirst into the spongy stem of a mushroom. I tried to call for help, but the gooey insides kept me from opening my mouth. All I could do was flail my paws in the air.

"He's stuck," I heard Thorn say. The next moment he, Civet and Indigo had pulled me free. But the cautious Shimmer was keeping one paw upon the lamp.

"Out of the way, if you please." She began to roll the lamp herself.

We trailed the dragon as she moved the lamp down the track toward the beach. The loud roar of the river soon announced that we were close to the shore.

Suddenly the white dog sprang out of the forest, red eyes glowing, fangs bared and looking twice as large as before. It had timed its leap so that it would barrel right into the jar and sweep it out from under Shimmer's paws and straight into a big boulder.

"No!" Shimmer cried, almost at the same time as the jar shattered.

CHAPTER SIXTEEN

With another bound of its legs, the dog disappeared back into the forest. Shimmer collapsed on her belly, her claws sifting through the shards. "There's hundreds of pieces. We can't glue them all together."

For the first time ever, Indigo looked as if she were on the verge of crying. "That mean old dog. If it wasn't going to get away, it wasn't going to let us get away either."

Shimmer thrust herself up from the ground and spun around, her lashing tail cutting a swath through a row of toadstools. "Monkey, this is all your fault."

With a nervous smile, I inclined my head to the glowering Civet. "At least I got you and Civet to agree on something."

Civet grabbed me from behind. "Shimmer, which part should we pull off first? A paw? His tail?"

"I swear that I tied that dog tight," I insisted.

Shimmer whipped her tail so that it cracked the air. "Let's start with his head. He'll never notice it's missing."

But Thorn thrust his arm between Civet and me. "We didn't get this far by blaming one another." Grabbing hold of Civet's hands, he pulled them away from me. "We have to work together."

"How?" Civet demanded. "Monkey's softheartedness may have cost us the only way off the island."

Unsure of what to say, the boy stood for a moment staring down at the pieces that now littered the trail. And then his head shot up. "There was only one big jar, but I saw a lot of small ones."

Shimmer kicked a shard out of the way with a hindpaw. "We can't work the magic to shrink down and fit inside them."

"Why can't we build a raft out of all the small jars?" Thorn asked, and he held out his arms in the outline of something large and square.

Shimmer's claw scratched her snout thoughtfully. "Yes, why not indeed?" And she looked over at me.

"Thorn's come through again," I whooped. Wrapping my arms around the boy, I bounced him off his feet.

But Civet cut the celebration short. "The dog's still loose," she said. "Let's gather up the jars right away."

We returned urgently to the courtyard of that strange, egg-shaped house, where we rounded up every jar that was there. "Empty them out," Shimmer directed. "No sense in carrying more of a load than we have to."

The jar I was holding felt light enough, but when I shook it, I heard a dry rustling inside—like autumn leaves scratching pavement. I turned it over, and something plopped onto the ground. It was a pink bundle; and when I bent to examine it, I saw the flat shape of a hand. Wiping my paw on my leg, I stared at it. "This looks like a human skin."

Civet came over. Having once been a Witch, she must have had a stronger stomach than the rest of us, because she prodded the bundle curiously with a toe. "Maybe this was one of the former guests of this island."

Thorn brought over a small metal pot. "I think it'll fit in here."

Civet frowned. "Leave it. The person's dead."

However, Thorn was determined to do the right thing. "You can go ahead; but this was once a person.

He or she deserves a decent burial." And he slipped the skin into the pot.

I pointed over to a spot among the flowerlike mushrooms. "That looks like a nice enough spot. Let me help."

"Harumph." Shimmer cleared her throat guiltily. "Better let someone dig who can create a proper grave." And going over to the patch, she scooped out the dirt with one big paw. And once we had placed the metal pot within the hole, even Indigo helped pack the dirt down on top.

Only Civet went on singlemindedly clattering through the junk as she hunted for more pottery. But from the corner of my eye, I noticed that she now turned the jars upside down once she found them. She wasn't going to have any more unpleasant surprises.

When Shimmer declared that we had done enough for the poor unfortunate, we started to load our arms up with jars and coils of rope. However, Shimmer shook her head at me. "Leave the load to the rest of us. You go ahead and keep an eye out for the dog."

Since that seemed sensible, I started forward into the air. But we had gone only about ten meters down the track when I heard something back in the courtyard. Looking over my shoulder, I saw the dog back by the house. "It's in the courtyard." I watched it sniff around. "It seems to be hunting for something, I think."

"We have all the jars," Civet declared with satisfaction.

At the beach Thorn set all his jars down except a small one. "Let's make sure the idea works before we start working on the raft."

All eyes were on the boy as he knelt by the water's edge and set the jar on the water. Then with a gentle shove, he released it. Bobbing up and down on the river currents, the little jar slowly drifted away.

I let out a whoop and cut a little caper on the sand. "Thorn's done it." And I pounded him enthusiastically upon his bony back.

Shimmer gave his shoulder a squeeze. "I'm glad one of us kept his head while the rest of us were losing ours."

Even Indigo gave him a quick, embarrassed hug. "You're really the clever one."

In his moment of triumph Thorn could afford to be gracious. "You would have thought of it eventually." Despite all his grievances against her, he couldn't seem to hold a grudge. I doubt if there was a mean bone in the boy's body.

Shimmer and I took turns keeping an eye out for the dog; but though we saw it lurking in the forest, it didn't dare try anything with us watching. In the meantime work went quickly as we lashed the jars together to form a raft some two meters wide on each side.

The only trouble was when it came time to launch the raft. While I kept guard, Shimmer began to ease the raft of jars through the sand. But as soon as the raft's edge touched the water, it stopped. Hind legs straining, she grunted, "I can't get this thing to budge."

"Help her," Thorn said, and squatted beside her to push at the raft. Anxiously Civet nudged Indigo, and they joined the dragon and the boy. But their combined efforts couldn't shift the raft a centimeter.

Thorn sat down exhausted and disappointed. "I don't understand it. The jar floated away."

Shimmer slapped at the sand in frustration. "This spell is more complicated than we thought."

"Maybe the spell works against a shape," I suggested.

But the boy sat there with his elbow perched on top of one knee and his chin resting on his fist. Knowing all eyes were on him, he plucked up handfuls of sand and let it trickle through his fingers while he thought. And suddenly his face lit up in that expression we had all come to know so well. "It's not the shape." He pointed at the ropes. "It's those things. It's threads twisted together like the reed boat. And that wouldn't float away, remember?"

Shimmer clucked a claw against the side of the raft. "Then how do we build a raft big enough to get the cauldron off the island?" she asked gloomily.

"And us," Civet added sourly. "Don't forget the rest of us."

Thorn pulled himself across the sand to the sack and took out the jar. "We've got glue." Untying one of the smaller jars, he put glue on its sides and, holding it by the neck, set it down on the water. "The only problem is if the spell affects the glue."

But as the jar floated away toward the falls after the first one, he raised the glue jar over his head proudly and declared, "It doesn't. We can build our raft."

Shimmer was already using her sharp claws to cut the ropes that bound the other jars. "Even if glue is strong enough, is there a sufficient amount to build a large raft?"

"We only need a small one to get us through the barrier." Thorn nodded to the hide pillow. "And some of our experiments would serve very well as floats. We could keep them on our laps until we're past the barrier and then use them when we get off and send the raft back for the next person."

As an experiment, we tried glueing just two of the jars together. They dried with amazing speed; and when Shimmer pulled at them, she grunted, "Umph. I wish I had the recipe for that glue. These two are joined together like iron."

However, we ran out of glue before we ran out of jars, and we had a raft only one meter square. I measured the raft and then eyed Shimmer's bulky body. "How are you going to get off the island? You can't shrink to fit the raft."

"Let's make sure." Shimmer turned so that her back was to both me and Civet. But when that spell proved as useless as all the others, Shimmer turned around once more, sadly toying with the gourd that she had tied around her neck. "I suppose you could always send help once you're off."

Myself, I would have done a little gloating after having been humiliated by the dragon. But Thorn was definitely a better person than I. He walked right over to his worried friend and crooked his finger at her.

"Have you got another one of your notions?" Shimmer hopefully craned her head down so Thorn could whisper in her ear. In a moment she was wagging her head excitedly, and then she looked over at me. "Would you care to make a wager about my leaving the island?"

I just shook my head at the grinning pair. "Not with Thorn helping you."

Civet selected a heavy stick of driftwood from the debris on the beach. "There's one precaution to take before we go." Standing up, she broke a spare jar and then looked at the rest of us defiantly. "We can't be sure if the dog and our host are innocent. If they are, I apologize to them. But we can't take chances— as you said. That dog might have another jar of glue around."

I sighed. "I'm less inclined to think they're innocent after finding that skin."

"It could have washed up inside the jar," Thorn pointed out.

"But our host picked it up. Why didn't he or she examine it like everything else?" Civet asked. "Why didn't our host bury the skin?" And she broke another jar.

Thorn stood there for a moment and then, bending over, picked up a stick. So did Indigo. And for a while it was silent on the beach except for the rhythmic breaking of pottery.

While we were busy helping Civet, Shimmer kept a watchful eye out. When the dog suddenly sprang out of the forest, Shimmer shouted, "Watch out." And she charged straight at it.

It halted on the edge of the beach, narrowing its red eyes and drawing back its lips in a snarl.

"Shoo." I did a series of bone-cracking kicks. "Shoo." And behind me the others all began to shout and wave their sticks.

Reluctantly, the dog took a step backward.

"We have to drive it away," Shimmer ordered without looking around. "We don't want it bothering us while we're leaving."

So we followed it, shouting and brandishing our weapons until it turned tail and fled back along the trail. "There," Shimmer declared with satisfaction, "I guess we showed it who's boss."

I watched the dog disappear among the fungus and scratched my chin. "Something's wrong. I mean, that was just too easy."

"Humph," Shimmer snorted. "Don't you think that we deserve a break for a change?"

"Maybe you're right," I admitted, and headed back to the beach. Once there, we quickly demolished the rest of the unused jars. And then Shimmer snatched up the hide pillow. "I think the first ride should go to the one who is responsible for our leaving the island." And she presented the pillow to Thorn.

With an elegant bow, I stretched out my arm. "Your yacht awaits you."

Embarrassed and yet pleased at the same time, Thorn sat down on the raft. When he saw the rest of us bending over to shove the raft into the water, he looked down at Civet. "This must have been what you saw in your vision."

"I saw what I saw," Civet grunted as she helped shove.

With the pillow on his lap, the boy sat proud as a little peacock while the raft slid out upon the water. The journey itself was only a few meters, but Thorn couldn't have smiled more proudly than if he had sailed around the world.

As he eased off the raft into the river, he gave a gasp. "It's cold. I'm glad I have the float." Clinging to it, he shoved the raft back in toward shore. Fortunately, the current wasn't strong here, because Thorn didn't have any trouble staying where he was.

I was next. Slowly I raised my elongated staff until it was standing upright on one end. Then, careful as an acrobat, I balanced it upright as I mounted the raft. When it cleared the barrier, I shrank my staff to toothpick size and tucked it behind my ear. "Free," I cried. "Free." And I did a series of somersaults that carried me into the air.

Civet was next, and she clung to a large piece of driftwood once she left the raft. But as Indigo got on the raft with another piece of driftwood, Shimmer took the gourd from around her neck and set it around Indigo's neck. "I'm trusting you with this," she said.

The words must have sent a pang through Thorn; but I leaned over to comfort him. "You were the first through the barrier. She didn't dare send it with you."

He nodded, sure that he had been restored to favor in general. But as Indigo proudly clung to her driftwood with the gourd in front of her, her hands were so full that Civet and I sent the raft back toward Shimmer.

As Civet bobbed up and down on the river, she said, "You're too big to sit on it. How are you going to use it to leave the island?"

Shimmer caught the raft with her paws. "This is Thorn's idea. When I was young, we used to do various exercises to get ready for flight. I never thought I'd have to do them again."

Shimmer held the raft steady with one forepaw.

Then, folding in her wings tight against her sides, she did a pawstand on her other forepaw. She stood there for a moment with one paw on the raft and the other on the beach.

The next moment, she had shifted both paws over to the raft. I held my breath while it wobbled along. "It's going to capsize," I warned.

"Don't say tha-a-at," Shimmer said as she toppled forward. She landed with a loud splash that sent spray over us. When we had blinked the water from our eyes, we could see her floating on her back and the raft bobbing beside her.

Though Thorn's legs must have been getting numb from the cold, he started to swim toward the raft. "Are you all right?"

A kick sent Shimmer outward into the river. "I'm fine. The barrier isn't a wide one."

I suppose as a dragon princess, she felt that she couldn't display her joy as openly as me; but even so she was inclined to feel a little frisky. Rolling over onto her stomach, she spread her wings, and with a sudden flap she rose into the air, dripping a regular rainstorm of water beneath her.

"We've got company," Indigo announced. I looked toward the beach and saw the white dog there.

Civet rose higher on top of her log. "Sink the raft," she said; but when I hesitated, she snapped, "Sink it. You can't afford to be sentimental."

Deciding that she was right, I shoved awkwardly at one side of the raft. It tipped just enough for the water to begin pouring into the jars. A moment later Shimmer was helping to lift the other end, and in no time our homemade raft had sunk beneath the water.

Back on the island the white dog raised its head and let out a howl that swept around the cavern like a lonely ghost.

And then it vanished once more into the strange, glowing forest.

CHAPTER SEVENTEEN

Shimmer glided toward the others, careful to keep from capsizing them. When she was only a few meters above them, she instructed them, "You must be getting cold. Grab hold of my tail and I'll give you a tow."

Banking, she curved around slowly and lowered her tail so that it cut a white wake behind her and helped to slow her down even more. As she passed, they took hold and let her pull them along through the water.

Quickly skimming driftwood from the river's surface, I landed just ahead of Shimmer on a narrow ledge a few meters above the river. Dumping my armload, I began to work a little fire spell. No one said anything, but I could feel anxious eyes watching me from the river. But to my relief—and everyone else's—the wet wood caught fire immediately, so that in no time there was a regular bonfire to welcome them from the icy water. As I felt the fire's warmth reach out to me, I felt even warmer inside that I could again work magic.

Banking once again in one of her smooth maneuvers, Shimmer brought them parallel to the ledge. Letting go of her tail, Thorn found a handhold on the stony wall beneath the ledge. But though his teeth were chattering, he paused as he pulled himself out of the water.

I got out my staff and stretched it out—a simple thing that I had missed in the short time we had been on the island. "Do you need help?" I asked him.

"I could have sworn that the sack moved funny after I let go—a kind of rocking as if someone else had gotten off too." He scrutinized the sack intently, but it was floating tranquilly as a current swept it toward the falls. Suddenly he leaned forward, almost slipping as he pointed. "There's a patch of white."

But when I craned my head forward, I could see only the dark river waters. "It was probably just some junk that sank."

In the meantime, Indigo had already crawled up onto the wall and was trying to drag her heavy log up after her. "Hey, how about giving me a hand?"

"Now that we can work magic again, even that log would burn," I agreed. After helping Thorn up onto the ledge, I helped her lift the log onto the ledge. Then we gave Civet a hand with hers.

With difficulty Shimmer landed a little bit farther down the ledge. For a moment she tilted as her claws scrabbled at the stone, trying to gain some purchase. But then she managed to get her balance.

"You're getting too fat," Indigo teased. "I think you ate too much on the island."

"They just don't make ledges like they used to." Shimmer sniffed and held her tail above the fire. Apparently the icy temperature had managed to penetrate even her hide. The dripping water hissed as it fell upon the fire.

"Careful, you're putting out the flames." I added the log to the fire. The wet wood began to send off streamers of steam, rising like a grove of ghostly saplings around the dragon's tail.

"The smoke will show us an opening. Green wood would smoke better," Thorn suggested, as he held out his hands toward the fire.

"No sooner said than done." I did a backflip that took me over the river.

In the meantime, while I was gathering wood, the fire must have taken the chill from Shimmer's tail, because she rose from the ledge and was circling far overhead.

"Hurry up, you little fur bag," she called down to me.

I was feeling too relieved to be insulted. Dumping the wood onto the bonfire, I shouted back to her. "I'm glad you finally found something useful to do, you overgrown hoptoad."

Soon real plumes of smoke began to rise. With a wave of my paw, I directed them so that they merged into a column of smoke. Shimmer didn't say anything, craning her neck to follow the rising smoke. It rose straight up from the ledge for some thirty meters until a current of air caught it and began to guide it toward the ceiling. Suddenly, the column of smoke began to wriggle like a hungry snake as it plunged into a crevice.

"Daylight, here I come," Shimmer announced, and threw herself after it.

Indigo was trying to wring the water from her clothes. "I've already lost track of time. Do you think it's still day outside, Thorn?"

Getting us off the island seemed to have raised his stock with her. Thorn had sat so he could keep one eye on the river for more wood. "I'm not sure—" he began. "There it is again," he said, pointing.

I saw a patch of white floating just beside the ledge. At first I was inclined to dismiss it as trash, but then

I thought I saw it move against the current. "Whatever it is, it looks like it's hunting for something."

Satisfying his curiosity must have been more important than staying dry, because Thorn plunged back into the river. But even as he tried to grab it, the thing dodged.

"Leave it," Indigo said, and stretched out her hand to help him back up.

"Got it." Thorn lunged, rising again with a splutter. "It's slick. And it feels kind of warm too." He raised the thing from the river. I noticed that it was almost pink—I suppose the river had made it look paler than it actually was.

As he held it up, it began to unroll like a narrow bolt of cloth. Thorn gave a gasp. "It's got arms and legs."

"It's another skin." Indigo slid back along the ledge.

Civet pressed her lips together thinly. "No, it's the same one."

Thorn held the object uncomfortably. "But we buried it."

Suddenly the eyelids rolled up on the flat face. The four of us found ourselves staring into a pair of eyes. "It's alive," Thorn cried, and dropped it.

"Grab it, you fool!" Civet said as she threw herself toward it. But Thorn was too horrified to move.

It took me a moment to overcome my own shock. And even as I rose into the air, the thing's arms had found a slender crevice, and the skin seemed to pour itself headfirst into the rock wall. By the time Civet had joined Thorn, the thing had already disappeared up to its knees.

"No!" Civet threw herself at the skin; but her fingers missed its toes by centimeters. And the next moment it had vanished into the rock. Desperately, Civet probed at the crevice, but even her fingers were far too wide to get into the crack into which the thing had gone.

Grabbing hold of Thorn by his collar, I hauled him up onto the ledge and dumped him by the fire. "Come back to the ledge," I said to Civet. "Whatever it is, it's gone now."

But Civet was clawing at the rock as if she would have torn the mountain down with her bare hands. "How many times do I have to tell you? I had visions, not nightmares. And now we've done it." She looked up at me desperately. "We've loosed the Great Evil."

I hovered over her uncertainly. "That thing?"

Civet stared bleakly at the stone where the creature had disappeared. "We should have been able to figure it out from the legends."

Indigo was staying beside the safety of the fire. "Who? What?"

"The Nameless One," Civet said sorrowfully. "The legends say that he was too powerful to be killed, so he suffered a fate that was too terrible to mention. But the clue was in the new name he was given—the name that was passed down to us."

I was just beginning to sense the magnitude of what we had done. "They stripped him of his powers and even his name. And they did that by stripping him of his shape. That's why there were no mirrors on the island—or anything that could show a reflection. The dog distracted us on the beach so that thing could crawl into a jar."

Indigo put a hand to her throat as she looked back at the island. "You mean that island was the prison for that awful wizard king?"

"That boneless creature was once a king," I said softly. "That's what made those odd marks. He wasn't covering his tracks. It was him crawling through the dirt."

And from one of the cracks above the ledge—as if he were already making his way up through the rock wall—there came a dry, crackling laugh, "Yes, the Boneless King, a new name for a new age."

Thorn began to pry at the cracks in the rock wall above the ledge. "We have to catch him."

Pulling hairs from my tail, I changed them into tiny monkeys. "Heaven help all of us. Out of the way, Thorn."

Thorn slid back on his knees so that I could send my children searching for the Boneless King.

"Too late, too late," the Boneless King taunted. "I'll make the entire world like the barrens—just as they made my land into these mountains."

A grim-faced Civet climbed back onto the ledge. "And now we've helped him to escape again."

As Thorn finally understood the enormity of what had just happened, he stared down at his hands. "No," he said. "It's not your fault. It's mine. It was my idea that helped him get free. And then I had him right in my hands, and I let him go."

Civet tried to comfort him. "You couldn't know."

"Well, he must still be powerless in this form," Indigo argued. "Or he would have done something to us rather than running away."

I began transforming one pawful of tail hairs after another. "Then we have to find him now—while he's still helpless."

Indigo shifted away from the puddle that was spreading from Thorn and Civet across the ledge. "How? This mountain seems honeycombed with crevices."

Cupping his hands around the sides of his mouth, Thorn shouted up toward the ceiling. "Shimmer, we need you."

Her voice floated down thinly from the top of the cavern. "I think I've found the way out." She gave a cough. "Drat that smoke. I feel like a ham that someone's curing."

But Thorn wasn't about to give up. "It's an emergency. The whole world could be destroyed."

Shimmer's sooty head poked out of a crevice skeptically. "Can't I leave Monkey out of my sight for a moment?"

Even so, she flew down to us, settling down with a frisky flip of her tail. But she sobered up quickly enough once we explained what had happened.

"We've loosed a terrible evil," I said, twitching my now bald tail. "We have to catch him now while he's still weak."

Shimmer hesitated, looking at the gourd that still hung around Indigo's neck. "Well, not all of us have to stay here. Someone should alert the Smith and the Snail Woman so they can inform the Five Masters."

My hairless tail was feeling cold, so I coiled it around my waist. "And no doubt that 'someone' would ask them to repair the cauldron at the same time."

Shimmer squared her shoulders defensively. "Well, why not?"

They say that dragons have one-track minds, so I knew it wouldn't do any good to beg her not to be so selfish. Instead, I tried a different argument. The Smith might not be so willing to fix it when he hears how we helped free the Boneless King."

"Boneless King?" Shimmer wondered.

"That's what he calls himself now," I said with a shudder.

Shimmer scratched the tip of her snout as if that would help her puzzle her way through the catastrophe. "Indeed? Well, yes, um, yes. You've had the most experience with the Snail Woman and the Smith. How do you think they'll take the news?"

"They don't have the sense of humor that my master has," I said.

Thorn hung his head. "If you need someone to blame, let it be me. It was my idea that helped him escape."

Reaching out a paw, Shimmer took his shoulder. "We all wanted to get off the island."

Thorn held up a hand. "But I had him and I let him go."

Her huge paw, meant for fighting rather than for signs of affection, caressed him clumsily. "Hush. It isn't necessary to take the blame."

Thorn shoved at the dragon's paw. "You said yourself that every day your clan is homeless, dragons die. Why should your clan suffer for what I did?"

"I will share whatever penalty is assessed by the Smith and the Snail Woman." Shimmer looked over at me. "How do I find the mountain of the Smith and the Snail Woman?"

"You can't really mean to leave," Civet objected. "The world could be at stake."

"He doesn't have any powers yet," Indigo argued. "We can be back in plenty of time with all the help we need."

"Or perhaps not," Civet said. "I'm staying."

"You made a vow—" Indigo began.

Shimmer held up a paw, regarding the former Witch coolly. "No, I won't stand in her way if she thinks it's important." She looked at me again. "How do I get in touch with the Smith and the Snail Woman? What's the signal you mentioned?"

Angry with the rationalizing dragon, I folded my arms. "And what if I didn't tell you?"

She lashed her tail in the air. "I would still go looking for them—and it would take me longer to return here."

"How can you be so selfish?" Civet demanded.

"That's a fine thing coming from you," Shimmer snapped. "And anyway, what's the world ever done for my people? Or for me?"

"I suppose it's no use discussing the matter?" I arched an eyebrow at the dragon.

She shook her head firmly. "My mind's made up."

I sighed. "As I recall, you burn the sap of a pine with twin trunks as a signal. And then you wait for them to come to you."

"Twin trunks?" Shimmer reared up in exasperation.

I shrugged. "It's not as if they like a lot of company."

Crouching on the ledge, Shimmer beckoned to Thorn and Indigo. "Hurry and mount up. We'll have to look for this miracle of modern communication. I'll fly you up there. If the crevice is wide enough for me, it'll be wide enough for you."

Clutching the gourd, Indigo got up, but Thorn

stayed where he was. "Don't dawdle," Shimmer scolded him impatiently. "We've wasted enough valuable time."

Thorn leaned miserably against the rock. "I can't leave without trying to set things to right."

Shimmer stamped a forepaw in annoyance. "I've had enough of that nonsense. It's not your fault. Now come along."

Thorn looked up at her. "No."

Shimmer spread a wing over the river meaningfully. "The ferryboat is leaving right this moment. Get on."

Thorn stared at her—no mean feat considering her eyes were half the size of his head. "Our place is here."

Shimmer seemed frustrated and even puzzled by her friend's resistance. "I thought you of all people would understand. What's gotten into you?"

Thorn glanced at me uncomfortably, and then he looked back at the dragon. He must have been remembering our conversation on the river, because though there was stress in his voice, there was also dignity. "Perhaps it's time to think on my own."

If Shimmer had been less proud, if she had begged Thorn to accompany her, he might have. As it was, she tried to resort to logic. "I don't expect Civet to keep her promises. But after everything we've been through, I thought you would."

Thorn spread his arms helplessly. "You know I wouldn't leave you unless I thought it was important."

"So be it." Shimmer swung her head away.

"Try to understand," he pleaded.

Refusing to look at him, Shimmer kicked herself from the ledge. "Oh, I understand quite well. You're just like all the rest—always let me down when I need you." With a nicely timed beat of her wings, she soared upward. "We'll be back as soon as we can."

Thorn raised his hand in farewell as she hovered, reluctant to leave. "Better disguise yourselves once you're out of the mountains. The soldiers might be around."

"We will." And with a sharp flap of her wings that sent the river water up in a spray, she rose away from the ledge.

I could only guess at what pain Thorn was feeling at that moment; but I imagine that it was as big as the cavern. As his eyes followed the soaring dragon, his lower lip began to tremble.

I put my arm around him encouragingly. "You're not alone. You've got us. Remember that."

But the boy cried anyway.

[*197*]

CHAPTER EIGHTEEN

We must have searched for about a day before I had to admit defeat. "With all the crevices and holes in this mountain, it's like looking for a grain of sand on a beach. I'd need a thousand times the monkeys I have."

"No, don't give up," Thorn insisted.

Civet finished the last of the fish that she had caught and that Thorn had cooked. "It's time to follow Shimmer and to warn the world."

I brightened up at that prospect. "Perhaps the humans and dragons would even arrange a truce. After all, the Boneless King is a threat to both humans and dragons."

Thorn's shoulders sagged. "So I could have gone with her anyway."

"You were trying to do the right thing." I tried to soothe him. When I had recalled all the little monkeys and returned them to my tail, I gave it an appreciative twitch. "I feel warmer already."

Then, with my shrunken staff tucked behind my ear, I carried Thorn up to the crevice Shimmer had found. After a meter it leveled off into a tunnel that paralleled the river, so I left him sitting there while I went back for Civet.

By the time I came back, I found the boy at the end of the tunnel, as if he were eager to be reunited with Shimmer.

"It's day," the boy called back happily.

"And a pretty narrow door," I said, studying the entrance. "That would force even a dragon to swallow her pride about proper sizes."

It was a slit perhaps half a meter wide and a meter high, and it looked as if brush had screened the mouth at one time—though the plants had been beaten down by Shimmer and Indigo when they had exited. And there were traces of icicles that had once hung down over the entrance like bars over a cage—though these were now snapped.

With Thorn still in the lead, we squirmed through the hole and out into the air. I took in deep, cold lungfuls. "I hope I never see a cave again."

However, Thorn had immediately begun to search around the entrance. "I don't see Shimmer's tracks."

I dipped my paw into the snow and felt how fresh and light it was. "It must have just snowed."

Thorn turned this way and that. "She could be anywhere."

Civet took his arm. "We'd better find the nearest settlement and alert them."

"Then a disguise might be in order for me," I said, and stroked my chin, wondering what might make a good display of my artistry.

"We'd be more likely to convince them with you in your true form," Thorn pointed out.

Remembering the ambush in the pass, I shook my head. "First, let's see which direction the wind is blowing in."

"And as long as we may be meeting soldiers, I should be careful too." Civet began to take off what jewelry had not fallen into the river.

I had just assumed the disguise of an old trader. "Unh-unh," I said. "What if we do encounter soldiers and they search you? You'll have to leave the jewelry behind."

"What if we need to buy something?" Civet held her small pile of jewelry in both hands.

"We'll come back for it," I swore.

But when Civet still hesitated, Thorn confronted

her. "Don't you remember your own vision? The important thing is to stop the Boneless King."

Thorn seemed to be able to make her listen more than anyone else could. She glanced down at her hoard. "With the world coming to an end, I suppose it really is silly to hold on to such things."

And before we could stop her, she flung up her arms, scattering jewelry all the way down the slope of the mountain, where it was lost in the glitter of the newly fallen snow. Breathless with exhilaration, she turned back to me. "There! Satisfied?"

More than anything else, that sacrifice convinced me that she believed in her own visions—though I still had my doubts about their accuracy. Even so, I merely scratched the tip of my nose. "You don't do anything by half, do you?"

She wriggled her shoulders. "I should have done that long ago."

Then, much lighter for jewelry, we began to make our way down from the mountain. We had come out on a shoulder of the mountain and had to angle through the snow toward the old caravan track.

The mountains rose all around us, steep and stark. "They say," I told Thorn, "that the Desolate Mountains were made when this country was tilted up during the war. That gives you some idea of the powers that were used."

"And now the Boneless King is loose again to start a new war," Thorn said unhappily.

A breeze lifted the newly fallen snow up in long streamers and veils that seemed to dance overhead. And the new snow crunched crisply under our feet.

Wind and sun had carved the snow into miniature peaked mountain ranges and valleys; and in places they had molded the snow into palaces with icy spires and turrets. And the thicker portions shone with a blue, jewellike light.

About halfway down the mountain the temperature got warmer, and there were strips where the snow had melted. Here and there odd snow mushrooms squatted—fat boulders resting on columns of snow. The sight of them reminded me of the island, and I couldn't help shuddering. All I could figure out was that some boulders had fallen off the mountain onto a huge drifts of snow. When the weather had begun to thaw, the snow had melted faster around the stone than underneath it, where it was shady.

And still farther down we came to fields of pebbles and boulders in the midst of which ice rose in gleaming pyramids some forty to fifty meters high. But these pyramids were turned upside down. Again, I suspected that when the thaw had come, the lower portions had melted before the higher mounds, resulting in the odd forest of giant white pyramids.

When we reached the caravan road, I estimated that it would take us several days before we reached a human settlement. However, we had no sooner rounded the next bend than we found ourselves in the middle of a entire platoon resting in a large alcove. And these weren't sloppy garrison troops like the ones in the Green Darkness. Beneath white camouflage cloaks the soldiers wore armor of red lacquered plates outlined in gold. Their steel, bell-shaped helmets gleamed with silver and gold decorations and their weapons were an ornate match. From the helmet of each soldier nodded tall, costly plumes.

These were soldiers dressed for show, and the only place they have such shows is in the palace. So I figured that they had to be palace guards. But what were they doing this far away from the capital and the war with the dragons?

Only something of vital importance would bring them up into the mountains, because the Butcher would never part with his special guards otherwise. More and more I realized that in coming into the mountains, we had flown straight into trouble.

Even so, despite their ornate armor, these were no toy soldiers. Tired as they must have been, they sat with rigid backs; and the scarves tied around their mouths hid their faces so that they all had the same anonymous look—as if they were all copies stamped by the same machine. The only difference between them was the irregular rising of steam when they exhaled through their scarves.

A sentry sprang forward, aiming a wickedly sharp spearhead toward my belly. "Lieutenant Crusher," he called.

A young officer, square as a wall, jumped to his feet. The plates of his armor clacked noisily as he raised a hand. "Halt."

As I saw the other soldiers raising their glittering spears as they got up, I spread out my arms to show that I was unarmed—or at least seemed to be. "We have to see your commanding officer immediately. The matter is very urgent."

"Oh? Is that a fact? Then you'd better come with me." The lieutenant used his free hand to gesture. "Corporal Tubs here is our tailor."

And a grizzled corporal with eyebrows like stiff

little brushes hurried forward with ropes. In the meantime Lieutenant Crusher continued on in the same amiable manner as before. "I hope you don't mind formal attire; but these are the general's orders."

They took away Thorn's dagger, but they missed the needle behind my ear—which suited me just fine. "Don't worry." I winked at Thorn as they bound my wrists. "Maybe a general will have more sense."

"A title doesn't make someone smarter," Civet sniffed.

"True enough," the lieutenant said, chuckling. "Now there's just a few more accessories to complete your outfit." And the officer tied his waist to mine with another length of rope, while Civet and Thorn were each tethered to a soldier. The lieutenant had slipped out a dagger and stepped in so close to me that I caught a whiff of his oiled, scented hair. "Oh, dear. I'm afraid that you're badly in need of a shave." And he set the dagger against my throat.

I was afraid to swallow with the sharp blade against my skin. "Thank you, but I prefer to do my own barbering."

"You've got enough nerve to be the spies we're looking for." But the lieutenant seemed to like my response, because he shifted the dagger so that it merely poked against my ribs. "So I really must insist. Anyway, it's orders for anyone we encounter up here." The lieutenant nodded, and Civet's and Thorn's guards also threatened them with daggers. "Now we'll return to camp slowly; and you should hope that I don't trip or my arm doesn't get tired."

Fortunately, the track was fairly level. About a half kilometer away they took a path that branched from the track up the cliffside. I moved as carefully as if I were made of fine crystal; and from the corner of my eye I saw that Civet and Thorn were walking with equal care.

When the path leveled off, we found ourselves on a plateau where strange, lumpy pillars rose some ten meters from the plain—as if an army of giants had been frozen in their tracks.

"What happened here?" Thorn wondered. "Is it more magic from the war?"

For a big man, the lieutenant moved nimbly enough. "You're as curious as my son." He nodded toward a small pool of water where steam rose. "This whole area is full of hot springs. Gradually, the minerals settle out of the bubbling water and form the pillars you see."

Here and there on the rocky plateau a geyser

would suddenly explode into life, sending up a huge cloud of steam toward the cloudy sky. And then there would be a hissing sound like a beached whale.

Eventually, though, we climbed up toward another ridge of hills through a pass filled with strange stone formations. And then, at the very top, we could suddenly look down on a valley where glittering little figures scurried like golden ants around what seemed like an anthill.

But as we descended down the pebbly path and I was able to gain a true perspective on things, I could see that the ants were really more guardsmen in their armor digging around a huge mound that sat in the middle of the valley floor. On one side trenches had been cut through centuries of accumulated dirt to reveal smooth black stones of basalt. Off to the side were row after row of white tents.

From the number of soldiers, I estimated that there was an entire regiment up here. Whatever their task was, it must be even more important than I had originally thought. But if the Nameless One should recover some of his power, all of them would be swept away like so many bugs.

Here and there were patches of snow on the valley floor; but strangely enough it felt colder than it had in the heart of the mountains. Or rather, it was a chill that seemed to go right into my bones, though I couldn't explain why.

And the feeling increased the closer we got to the mound. By then I had begun to appreciate its size. It rose for some forty meters into the air like some giant's skull. At the base was a mouthlike hole some four meters high and just as many wide. And patches of snow clung to its sides like bits of dead skin.

Before the mound was a huge pit some fifty meters square. And in the middle of the pit were a hundred men standing absolutely still.

"Are they dead?" Thorn asked the lieutenant.

"Full of questions, aren't you? Just like a good little spy." However, the lieutenant seemed inclined to indulge the boy. "No, they're statues."

As we neared the pit, I could see that they were stone statues, each of a soldier in antique armor and weapons, and each face seemed to be different from the others—as if they were taken from individual models. But I wished I had Shimmer's sharper eyes to make sure.

Around the edges of the pit, guardsmen were excavating more statues under the watchful eyes of robed, furred wizards.

"Why did someone bury so many statues?" Thorn wondered.

The lieutenant smiled quizzically at Thorn as if he were beginning to entertain genuine doubts about his being a spy. "It's not my usual subject matter"— the lieutenant shrugged—"but a wizard told me that long ago people used to do that when they buried a king or queen."

By now we were standing in the shadow of the huge mound. "Then this is someone's burial site," Thorn said in awe.

I thought of the toys that had been buried with the sorceress in the crypt under the lake. From the size of the burial, the person here must be someone very important indeed.

Next to the excavation site blue-robed wizards stood before tables as they pored excitedly over ancient scrolls. Other tables were piled with dirty jars and pots bubbling on coal braziers.

When I smelled the smoke, I knew that they had found alchemical books as well as statues. (My master had once explained alchemy as one of the natural arts, but with more practical uses than most branches of magic.) From the looks of things, they were busy experimenting with the recipes in the scrolls.

The odd thing was that the mud here was blackened as if by fire, but the ground was twisted into odd shapes. However, when I started to stare, the lieutenant pressed the point of his dagger against my side. "Hurry up there," he ordered. "You can buy a ticket for the circus later."

But the next moment a wizard gave a cry and jumped back from a table. With a soft *whump*, the air was filled with a terrible odor and the table itself was hidden in a dense cloud of smoke.

Everyone began coughing, guards and prisoners alike. "It smells like all the rotten cabbage in the world," I complained.

Blue-robed wizards stumbled out of the cloud, their arms filled with pieces of equipment or armfuls of scrolls and cylinders—and looking for all the world like ants when their home is flooded.

The lieutenant studied the direction in which the wizard's robes were flapping. "So much for the secrets of the ancients. The wind seems to be blowing right toward the wizards' section of camp." And he broke into a broad, satisfied smile—so I gathered that there was no love lost between the guardsmen and the wizards. Maybe the soldiers blamed the wizards for their being stuck up here.

"Isn't that a pity," one of the guardsmen growled in a very satisfied way.

Keeping the dagger on my side, the lieutenant led

us into a section of tents into whose sides ventilation holes had been cut so that they were more like pavilions than tents.

I wrinkled my nose disdainfully at the pungent chemical smells filling the air. The place reeked of strong chemicals; and through the ventilation holes I could see long, low tables where nervous guardsmen seemed to be mixing chemicals and filling black earthenware jars before they sealed them with plugs of clay. When each jar was finished, it was put into a basket of straw.

At the entrances to the tents were wizards keeping tally as soldiers staggered out with baskets full of the black jars, taking them to a large, heavily guarded tent that must have been some kind of warehouse. In front of that tent was another team of wizards keeping their own tally. Whatever was in the jars, the wizards didn't want to lose one of them.

An elderly wizard in blue robes with purple symbols was gesturing toward the procession of baskets. "But you can smell what just happened," the wizard was protesting. "We're not sure what all the symbols in the scrolls mean. We have to study them and experiment, General Winter."

General Winter listened to the scolding with thinly disguised contempt. He was in white armor with gold-leaf decorations all around—so much gold, in fact, that he looked like a lobster that had rolled in gold dust. "Would you care to discuss the delay with His Highness?"

The elderly wizard swallowed, apparently at a loss for words.

"Sir." The Lieutenant cleared his throat.

General Winter pivoted smartly on his heel as if he had lost none of his drill and polish and scrutinized us intently.

I took a step forward, but the lieutenant caught at the rope and hauled me back. At the same time he brought the blade up against my throat. "Halt."

But I decided to take the risk. "General, there is a terrible evil loose." I remembered to use the old name for the Boneless King. "The Nameless One is free in the mountains."

General Winter folded his arms across his chest with a faint clacking sound. "Oh? And so are five dragon spies."

"What the Nameless One can do," I argued, "is far worse than any harm the dragons could."

"How interesting," General Winter said. "And you say he's wandering around the mountains again?"

"But with all your troops you might be able to find him," I explained.

General Winter rocked up and down on the balls of his feet. "Well, if the Nameless One is alive and roaming around, then who is in his tomb?" And the general swung one arm up to point at the mound.

Instinctively, I turned to look back at that skull-like mound; but a poke of the dagger made me face the general again. "Have you found his body yet?"

General Winter glanced at the wizard. The elderly man puffed himelf up within his magnificent robes. "No, but his name is all over the tomb."

I stomped one foot in exasperation. "It was prepared for his burial, but he was never buried there. The Five Masters couldn't destroy him. We've been trapped in the spot where he really was imprisoned."

General Winter frowned. "If you want to start a panic, you'll have to come up with a better story than that." He waved his hand. "Take them away and hold them with the other prisoners until I can question them further."

Curious about the identity of the other prisoners, I let the lieutenant lead me away. But once that curiosity was satisfied, I intended to come back and unshell that pompous lobster.

CHAPTER NINETEEN

We were led through a large camp of white tents. Somehow the Butcher had found the location of the Nameless One's tomb—perhaps it was some diligent wizard poring through dusty archives. In any event, the Butcher must have heard of some secret buried in the tomb that made it worthwhile to come up here and dig. I suppose it was the wizards who had laid the traps with the nets in the canyons.

We were taken to a large, white tent that was surrounded by a squad of the same resplendent guards. None of them looked very happy at having to stand out in the snow and the wind; and from their glowering expressions, they seemed to think it was our fault.

Two hermits, an older one in a green robe and a younger, shorter one in blue, sat inside with their arms bound behind their backs. A soldier was stationed behind each, holding a dagger by his throat. They looked up sharply when we came in, and the one in the blue robes glanced down meaningfully at the gourd that hung around his neck, so I knew he was Indigo and the older, taller one was probably Shimmer. I suppose they had taken Thorn's advice to disguise themselves before they left the mountain.

I looked a silent question at them. But the one in the green robe gave a slight shake of his head. Apparently they hadn't contacted the Smith and the Snail Woman—though I couldn't tell whether they had not been answered or if they had even gotten off a signal at all.

We were forced to sit down in a row next to Shimmer and Indigo, where we were also kept at dagger point—though Lieutenant Crusher and his men took turns, the ones off duty using the time to polish their armor and weapons. (That wouldn't have been my choice after a hard tramp through the Desolate Mountains, but then guardsmen do a lot of silly things.)

The platoon had just finished putting themselves to rights when we heard horns bleating odd, deep notes like pregnant goats, and a staff officer ordered us outside again. When we were lugged out of the tent, still at dagger point, I had to blink my eyes.

In front of the camp the guard was drawn up in row after row, each soldier glittering like a miniature sun with reflected light. Feeling especially shabby, we were dragged through the haughty ranks to join a shining company of officers. There were courtiers there too in expensive, padded silk robes bright as any parrot.

We had just been lumped at the tail end of the assembly when horns sounded their strange notes again from in front of a huge white tent from which golden pennants fluttered.

"You'll have to adjust your height like the rest of us," the lieutenant said amiably. The frozen earth was hard as stone as we knelt with the rest of the assembly.

"What's this?" a deep voice boomed from overhead. "A circus in the mountains?"

I had been busy looking for someone to come up the path. Now when I craned my head back, I saw a dragon hovering in the air. For a moment I thought it was Shimmer. But then I realized that the dragon didn't have enough scars to be her.

Next to me Shimmer gasped, and I couldn't help glancing at her. But there she was herself, gazing up at the sky.

"What's going on?" the lieutenant demanded suspiciously.

Quickly recovering, Shimmer bowed her head. "I have never seen a dragon before—that's all."

On the back of the dragon was a man as round as a barrel. His armor had been tailed to fit his torso; and yet except for the large jewel around his throat, the armor was plainer than the guardsmen's equipment. Nor did he seem to have any neck. Rather his lumpy head seemed fused to his thick body; and his squashed features looked as if someone had taken a dog and mashed in its face. Even so, I thought that there was something familiar about him.

As soon as the dragon landed in the mud, soldiers instantly ran forward and threw themselves, glittering armor and all, into the mud, forming a shining path directly to us. Sliding off the dragon, the barrellike man strode over the soldiers' backs toward us, oblivious of the grunts that came from the living road as he walked.

Behind him the dragon raised a forepaw. "You promised as soon as we landed."

The man pivoted, forcing one guardsman deeper into the mud. "Cross me and you won't have it at all."

Rising with now-muddy trousers, the general bowed low. "Your Highness, we have just captured five suspicious persons who might be the dragon spies."

When I heard General Winter address the barrellike man in that manner, I knew where I had seen him. His image was on every newly minted copper coin. It was the Butcher himself. Licking my lips, I called to him urgently, "You have to believe us. The Nameless One is loose in the mountains."

When General Winter shot a dirty glance at me, the lieutenant grabbed the back of my head. "You crazy old loon, now you've done it." And he tried to force my face into the mud.

But I resisted because I wouldn't have been able to speak with a mouthful of mud. "You have to listen to me. The whole world could be destroyed."

"Quiet," the lieutenant whispered fiercely. "You'll just make it worse for yourself."

"Let him be," the Butcher ordered. When I looked up, I saw the general whispering in the Butcher's ear. And then, as the king leaned over me curiously, his face as big and round as a moon, "Your lies won't help you, spy. What are you really afraid of?"

I have faced all sorts of monsters without blinking, but there was something about his smile that unnerved even me. "Wha-a-at do you mean?" I stammered.

The Butcher straightened up. "The problem in dealing with dragons is that they can take any shape."

"These two"—General Winter indicated Civet and Thorn—"were his companions."

The Butcher nodded. "Then the other two will be hostages for his good behavior. At the first sign of trouble, kill them."

"But we came to warn you," I protested.

However, the Butcher didn't believe me any more than General Winter had. "Tell me how you knew to come here. Confess, and I might permit you and your companions to die quickly."

Behind him, the dragon called to the Butcher, "Please."

But though the Butcher stiffened, he tried to ignore the creature. "I myself will take a hand in your questioning." The Butcher smiled even wider—and I realized what bothered me about his grin. He was someone who enjoyed other people's pain.

Next to him, I saw, General Winter suppressed a shudder as if this were not the first time that the Butcher had helped out.

"Pretty please," the dragon wheedled.

Exasperated, the Butcher whirled around. "Have some dignity for once."

But the dragon was crawling shamelessly on its belly through the mud. "I'm begging you."

"You have no sense of the occasion," the Butcher scolded the dragon.

I think any human would have tried to hide from that regal glare; but the dragon was too desperate to be afraid and kept right on crawling. "A true king would keep his promises."

The Butcher stiffened as if he were sensitive about his pedigree. "Oh, very well." Striding back over the living road to the dragon, he flipped up the flap of the saddle bag that hung over the dragon's back. "He must have some place that's private," he said to the general.

General Winter hid his surprise by bowing. "He may use my tent, Your Highness."

With a grunt, the Butcher lifted out a flat, oval object about two thirds of a meter in length. It was wrapped in gold silk; but as he took it from the saddle bag, one of the corners fell, revealing a shiny bronze surface. "Your problem is that you have no discipline."

A company of soldiers instantly formed a detour to the general's tent—a large, cone-shaped one. And when his new path was ready, the Butcher strode toward it with General Winter accompanying him on one side and the dragon on the other, waddling with pathetic eagerness.

As the assembly broke up, a soldier turned to Corporal Tubs. "I don't care if that dragon is his pet. Like should stay with like; and no good comes of mixing with that breed."

"Quiet, Slowfoot," the lieutenant hissed. "You never know who might hear you. Do you want to be arrested as a traitor?"

Slowfoot didn't say anything, but his face grew pale under his helmet. Satisfied that his man had learned his lesson, the lieutenant twitched my rope. "Come on. You have to get ready for His Highness' tea party." As he led us through the camp, he advised us seriously, "If you know anything, I'd tell it now. His Highness didn't get his nickname for the quality of his penmanship."

As I made a pretence of strolling along like someone with a clear conscience, I checked the tents ahead of us for some opportunity for escape. "You seem like a reasonably decent sort. How can you serve someone like him?"

The lieutenant hesitated and then shrugged one shoulder. "He keeps order."

"Harsh as it seems to be," Civet corrected him.

The lieutenant was grim faced. "With the royal family gone, we faced anarchy and civil war. Everyone would have suffered then."

"Instead of a few," Civet pointed out.

"As you like," the lieutenant said, and wouldn't be baited anymore. When we reached a tent at the very end of the camp, he threw back the flap.

Instantly warm air blew in our faces. And as we stepped inside, we found a charcoal brazier blazing away, giving off such heat that the man inside had stripped down to the waist. He looked almost as furry as me. "I knew there'd be work for me as soon as His Highness came. That's why I got the fire going."

"How thoughtful," I said. "I think this is the first time I've been warm since I've come into the Desolate Mountains."

"Let's just hope it won't be your last," the lieutenant said. At his direction, I was clamped to a chair. When he was satisfied I could not get away, the lieutenant loosed the ropes that bound me.

When the man turned, his back was just as hairy as his front. "You're like all the rest. You look at a few thugs, and you judge all of us the same way.

But it's a profession, you see. And there are standards to uphold."

"Torture?" Civet asked as a guard took up a position behind her with a drawn dagger.

"Ah, now, you see, that's just the kind of prejudice I have to fight all the time." The hairy man took a leather apron from a camp chair and began to put it on. "I'm a facilitator, specializing in information retrieval."

"And what's that?" Thorn asked as he was positioned next to Civet.

"A torturer," Civet grunted.

The hairy man looked genuinely pained. "Facilitator, please." He checked the clamps about my wrists. "Now then. That's not too tight, is it? Blood getting through to your little piggy-wiggies?"

"Unh, yes." I wriggled my fingers and toes in illustration.

"He wouldn't want you going numb," Civet snapped.

The facilitator sounded hurt. "I don't see why you shouldn't be comfy until we begin." Humming to himself, he began to place the tips of various tools in the brazier.

"Better wait for the Butcher," I said.

"Not again." The facilitator shot an annoyed look at Lieutenant Crusher.

The officer shrugged. "His Highness has taken a personal interest in . . . unh . . . retrieving some information."

"Amateur," the facilitator muttered under his breath.

All too soon the Butcher swept into the tent. "Ah, nothing like a cheerful fire on a cold day." Shedding his furred cloak, he tossed it to the guardsman called Slowfoot while the facilitator held out another leather apron for him. But the Butcher ignored him when he saw me in the chair. "Idiots, begin with the boy." He smiled again at me. "So this old fellow can see what's in store for him."

As a stiff-legged Thorn was led toward the chair, the Butcher slipped the apron over his own head. "You look more used to that apron than to a crown," Civet sneered.

The Butcher stiffened as if stung and then forced himself to calmly finish tying on his apron. "It's no secret. When I was young, I made my living by cutting up cattle into steaks. But I learned a thing or two while the soft folk were lolling around in their palaces."

"How to roll in blood," Civet supplied.

"How to get what I want." The Butcher began to roll up the silk sleeves of his tunic.

As the lieutenant took out the key to unclamp me from the chair, I couldn't understand why Civet was deliberately goading the Butcher. And then it hit me that she was trying to draw his attention to herself rather than to Thorn. Perhaps she thought the flames in the brazier had been predicted by her vision.

The Butcher went brusquely over to the brazier. Hastily, the facilitator backed away, bowing with each step. "You're awfully eager to protect the boy."

I got ready in the chair, preparing to charge. But the lieutenant was too cautious. At a nod of his head, Tubs held a dagger again at my throat, so that I would have no choice but to let them tie me up as soon as I was free from the clamps.

Pulling on a pair of heavy leather gloves, the Butcher selected a pair of red-hot tongs. "Tell me your mission," he asked Civet, "and I'll simply imprison you."

"Why is it that I don't trust you?" she asked.

The Butcher spat on the end of the tongs and saw his spittle hiss instantly into steam. "You don't have much choice." He started to point the tongs at Civet; but then with a malicious grin he continued on until they stopped near Thorn. "I'll still begin with the boy. Perhaps it will make these others confess eventually."

But I should have known that a dragon would pay back her debts.

"Wait," the disguised Shimmer said. "I'll tell you what you want to know."

The Butcher spun about. "I'm glad that someone has some sense."

And as the Butcher stood before her, Shimmer said very firmly, "You were probably a bully when you were a little boy; and your manners haven't gotten any better." And she spat at him.

CHAPTER TWENTY

There was dead silence inside the tent for a moment. And then there was the hiss of swords sliding from sheaths as the guardsmen began to draw their weapons.

However, the Butcher put up his free hand. "Hold your positions." Calmly he began to wipe his face. But a muscle was twitching in his cheek. "Congratulations. You've just moved to the head of the line."

I think that that was exactly what the dragon had intended—though in her human form she was just as vulnerable as any human. Even so, Shimmer bowed her head in mock humility. "I am a mere hermit. I'm unworthy of the honor."

The Butcher didn't answer. He simply stood there studying her while the tongs cooled in his gloved hand. We could hear excited shouts outside; but he ignored them, focusing on the disguised dragon.

"For someone facing torture, you don't seem very afraid."

Shimmer dipped her head contritely. "I've been taught how to control my feelings."

"Except for contempt." The Butcher clicked the tongs open and shut several times. "Could you be planning to change into something green and deadly?" He glanced at the lieutenant. "Be especially alert. At the first suspicious move from him, kill the others."

"But Your Highness," Shimmer insisted, "if I were truly a spy, would I call attention to myself? As I said, I'm only a humble hermit."

The Butcher spun on his heel and dumped the tongs back into the brazier. "That raises another problem then. Perhaps you really are what you say. But then how do I punish you for that insult? I've heard of hermits who have gained magical powers. Perhaps you're impervious to fire." The Butcher yanked off his gloves and tossed them to the facilitator. "But is there some element you're afraid of? Water? Metal? Wood? Earth?"

Indigo, though, had kept her wits, and she picked up on the ruse and began to play along. "I'll tell you. Just let me go."

Shimmer turned around and pretended to be angry. "Silence. You're my disciple."

"I'm tired of the mountains," Indigo snapped. "And I don't want to die."

At a nod from the Butcher, the guardsman behind Shimmer pressed a dagger against her throat so that she was forced into a sullen silence. Through the thin tent walls came the sound of trumpets bleating out the alarm; but we were all watching the Butcher swagger over toward Indigo. "Tell me what I want to know, and I'll spare your life and let you be a slave."

"But—" Indigo began.

"You'll like the alternative even less." The Butcher jerked his head toward the torture instruments in the brazier. "Life is a series of hard choices, isn't it?"

Indigo gulped and pretended to hang her head in shame. "He's afraid of earth," she mumbled.

And suddenly I could see Indigo's little game. Shimmer always took a moment to change into a dragon. But if she were buried in the dirt, she could hold her breath long enough to change safely and then rescue us. I could just picture her bursting out of the dirt and in the confusion freeing us.

However, the Butcher was no fool. He narrowed his beady little eyes. "Are you sure he isn't our dragon?"

The next moment the tent flap was thrown back and a guard poked his head in. "Your Highness, the general urgently requests your presence."

"I'm busy." The Butcher glowered.

But though the guard started to tremble, he stayed stubbornly where he was. "It's an emergency."

"Oh, very well." The Butcher took his cloak from Slowfoot; and, as he pulled it on over his apron, he nodded to the lieutenant. "And see that this fool"—he indicated the messenger—"loses his head. Emergency or not, he's too persistent for my tastes."

Reluctantly Lieutenant Crusher nodded; but the Butcher was already pushing past the now terrified guardsman. As he stood there, the lieutenant nodded resignedly to Tubs. "Take his weapons."

As the corporal was disarming the messenger, another guardsman bustled into the tent. "We've caught something trying to sneak into the tomb. His Highness wants the prisoners to see if they can identify it."

With daggers threatening us still, we were led slowly outside. The whole camp seemed to be in an uproar as troops double-timed this way and that while the second messenger led us toward the tall mound. Just before the pit of statues we saw a circle of some hundred guards with torches in one hand and weapons in the other.

The Butcher, who had been keeping an eye out for us, beckoned a hand. When we were lined up before him and General Winter he explained, "Swords won't cut it. Spears won't pierce it. Arrows bounce off it." Impatiently the Butcher shoved several guardsmen out of the way. "I'll release the person who can tell me what this thing is."

There, in the center of the ring, was the stretched-out skin of a man. I might have thought he was a paper cutout; but he whirled first to his left and then to his right like a trapped animal. The only sound he made was a rustling noise—like paper being crumpled up.

I had seen it before in Egg Mountain. "That's the Nameless One," I insisted. "Now will you believe me?"

"The Nameless One was once the fairest of humans," the Butcher said skeptically. "That boneless thing isn't even human."

"How dare you?" A funny, squeezed kind of voice came from the skin stretched out on the mud. "Thief, burglar, fool."

The Butcher hesitated. "Are you really the Nameless One?"

The creature on the ground tried to draw itself up proudly; but a breeze kept knocking it back into the mud. "Yes. But I am nameless no longer; for I am the Boneless King." He seemed to take delight in the shudders that name produced among the surrounding soldiers. "And this tomb is mine. Let me enter, and I will give you more power than you ever dreamed of."

I pointed warningly at him. "Don't trust him. Right now he can't work any magic. But once he gets whatever he's looking for, we're all done for. Destroy him now."

"Why would I lie to a fellow king?" the Boneless King demanded.

The Butcher whispered something to General Winter, who left instantly. Then he turned back to the Boneless King. "What you say may be true, my royal filet. But if there is any magic in the tomb, it's mine already, and so is the power."

"Fool! Your puny mind could never understand my magic. When I'm done with you, the only thing people will remember about you is the gruesomeness of your death." And he began to creep forward on paper-thin fingers.

Jerking a spear from a guardsman, the Butcher handed it to the condemned messenger. "Stop him."

Bravely, the messenger advanced with the spear thrust out toward the Boneless King. When he was within range, the messenger stabbed down, but the spearhead slid magically from the Boneless King's skin.

And then the King arched up in a fluid curve. Flattened hands gripping the spearhead, the Boneless King pulled himself up the spear shaft, almost flowing along the wood.

At first the messenger stood there in shock. By the time he tried to drop the spear, it was already too late; for the Boneless King rippled forward to cling to his chest. "Help me," the panicked messenger screamed. His hands slapped and shoved in vain at the Boneless King.

But it was like trying to throw away taffy. The Boneless King stuck to the poor messenger; and gradually his hands found the hapless man's throat.

Lieutenant Crusher, unable to stand the spectacle any longer, handed my rope to Tubs. "Guard him."

As Tubs drew his own dagger to use against me, the lieutenant shoved between the other trembling guardsmen. Dagger in one hand and sword in the other, he marched up to the Boneless King. But he couldn't slash at the Boneless King without also hurting his victim, who was now lying on his back. As he hovered helplessly nearby, the Boneless King slowly strangled the poor messenger.

At that moment General Winter returned with one of those odd, globelike jars. Scurrying indignantly at his heels was the elderly wizard. "I really must protest. It's much too early to test the bomb."

The Butcher motioned Lieutenant Crusher to him. "Either it works or it doesn't. But you had better pray that it does, or you'll be shorter by a head."

As the elderly wizard stood there nervously rubbing his throat, the Boneless King had finished choking his victim and was crawling off the corpse toward the Butcher.

"Destroy that thing," the Butcher ordered the lieutenant.

Whatever else he was, Lieutenant Crusher was no coward. Sheathing his sword and dagger, he took the bomb from General Winter and marched into the ring as if he were in a parade.

"Out of my way, fool," the Boneless King crackled.

Lieutenant Crusher stopped as still as a statue, waiting as the Boneless King crept straight toward him. The King's flat legs dragged over the frozen mud with a hissing sound like a snake slithering through the dirt. The sound alone would have sent me running even without the threat of the weird creature. But the lieutenant stood there at attention.

When the Boneless King was only a meter away, he began to reach out for the lieutenant's ankles. "Now," the Butcher commanded.

Quickly the lieutenant dropped the jar on top of the Boneless King. It shattered with a crash; and for a moment the creature lay there. Then, with a harsh laugh, he heaved himself up again, shaking off the fragments.

Drawing his sword again, the lieutenant took a cautious step back. "Fool." The Boneless King gave his strange laugh. "Your toys can't save you."

But suddenly little plumes of smoke began to rise from the back of the Boneless King. "No," he cried in surprise, "you couldn't have found it already."

It was the Butcher's turn to gloat. "Yes. We know the secret of your living fire."

Little tongues of flame erupted along the back of the Boneless King like bright little nails. Desperately, the Boneless King flipped himself onto his back and tried to roll to put out the flames. It wasn't magic but a chemical reaction. And he no sooner extinguished one area than flames burst out once again as soon as it was exposed to the air. The heat from the flames began to thaw out the earth, which quickly turned into mud. Flapping like some paper cutout caught in the wind, the Boneless King tried everything he could to save himself; but the fire kept spreading.

The wizard beamed proudly. "I knew all the time that it would work."

Surprised, I couldn't help looking at the still-disguised Shimmer. "It burns even in the wet mud."

"I'll bet it would burn even in water," Shimmer said in horror.

"But you have matches that burn under the sea," Thorn blurted out.

Shimmer shook her head. "That's magic. This is something else."

The Butcher had been keeping an eye on us all the while. "So you *are* a dragon spy. Perhaps even a dragon itself." He smiled at Shimmer. "By the time your mages realize that this is chemical rather than magical and take the proper steps, it will be too late. I'll have already turned your seas into flaming hells. But that knowledge won't do you much good." He nodded to the wizard. "Fetch another bomb so we can test it on a dragon now."

Suddenly from the middle of the fire rose a high scream that grew louder and louder until we were all covering our ears. The next instant a pair of burning arms flapped in the air like a pair of shirt sleeves on fire.

Slapping his fat thighs, the Butcher laughed. "Burn, you monster."

But at that instant a blue ball of light flashed from the Boneless King and into the air. Whizzing about like a mad comet, it darted through the air straight toward the Butcher.

"No!" the Butcher cried, and threw up his arms to protect himself. But the ball of light smashed against his chest, knocking him to the ground.

CHAPTER TWENTY-ONE

Anxiously, the officers and courtiers gathered around the fallen Butcher even as the flames finally began to burn themselves out in the mud, the chemical reaction having run its course.

While my guard was distracted, I grabbed the wrist of his knife hand and jumped up. I had already estimated the differences in our heights, and my skull caught him neatly beneath the chin. He was falling backward unconscious while I took a step over to Thorn.

He'd had the presence of mind to shove his guard's dagger away from his throat. One punch from me and his guard fell on top of his comrade. I heard a grunt from my right and turned in time to see Civet's guard rolling back and forth in the mud and clutching his belly. With an unceremonious kick to his head, Civet laid him out cold.

In the meantime Shimmer was holding the knife hand of her captor while she swung her free elbow behind her to his throat. He made a choking sound, but even before he had fallen to his knees, she was swinging over toward Indigo. The girl had already seized her guard's wrist in both her hands and was biting it—fortunately, his screams went unnoticed in the general hubbub.

A blow from Shimmer's left hand felled him, and a blow from her right hand knocked out her own guard. She rubbed the sides of her hands. "Now to pay them back." Then her lips began moving as she transformed herself into her true form.

As I took my place by her, Civet, Indigo and Thorn took daggers and swords from their former guards. Though I doubted the children knew how to use them, they certainly looked fierce.

But they hardly needed to bother arming themselves, because everyone was still busy with their fallen king. As I changed myself into my true shape and expanded my staff, Shimmer shook out the kinks in her joints from having stretched herself into true shape. I noticed, though, that she had changed to a length a little longer than the other dragon. The next moment she had changed Indigo back.

Thorn looked over at me. "Is the Boneless King really dead?"

"There was that ball of light," I said, "so I can't say for sure." Wishing my master were here, I glanced over at the crowd around the Butcher.

From the middle of the mob, I heard the Butcher shouting, "I'm all right. Get away." Immediately, courtiers, officers and soldiers began backing up, and we saw him standing with his chest puffed out and pumping an arm. "In fact, I feel better than ever." But he looked like someone trying on a new shirt.

"A dragon!" a soldier shouted. "A dragon!"

Annoyed, I jumped up so that everyone could notice me as well. "And also the Great Sage Equal to Heaven," I shouted back.

"Quick, climb on," Shimmer ordered the others.

The Butcher, however, seized the nearest wizard, a little man with a goatee done up like a corkscrew. "Take away their powers of flight."

"But Your Highness, even I, Horn the Incredible, know of no such spell," the little wizard protested.

Gripping him by the back of the neck, the Butcher shook the little wizard like a dog shaking a rat. "Try, or I'll snap your scrawny neck."

Horn the Incredible was so badly frightened that he could barely raise his arms, and his goatee shook while he began a quavering chant. But behind him we could see the Butcher moving his lips as if he were whispering a spell himself.

"I've had enough of the royal hospitality." Spreading out her great, leathery wings, Shimmer gave a flap that should have sent her soaring into the air, but instead she remained earthbound.

Horn seemed as startled as Shimmer as he lowered his arms. But behind him the Butcher was smiling ominously.

I recalled the curse that had been placed upon the Boneless King. "When he was stripped of his shape," I said, "he was stripped of his powers."

Shimmer had the same horrifying thought. "But now that he has a new shape, he has his powers back."

And the Boneless King spread his arms out as if to say that he did, indeed, have his powers back. "That's not the Butcher," I cried to the guardsmen. "That's the Boneless King, I mean the Nameless One. He's taken over the king's body."

All the recent magic had undone their usual discipline, so they looked uncertainly at one another. But then General Winter, feeling bolder now that he had seen magic stronger than ours, strode forward. "That is the Nameless One." He pointed at the patch of ashes. "You can't trick us."

Civet slipped off Shimmer back to the ground. "Take the children away. I think I know the spell. It's an old one and works only so long as the caster of the spell can see you. Find the Smith and the Snail Woman."

Thorn almost fell over as he stretched out his hand to catch her. "Where are you going?"

For the first time since I had met her, Civet seemed almost at peace. "Remember this when it is your own time," she said to him. "We may live our lives as we like; but there will come a day when we are asked to pay the price. I don't know how, but you will have great powers someday. Accept it." And then she had pulled free of Thorn and darted behind Shimmer. "I now pay my debt to you and your people," she called to the surprised dragon.

General Winter sent a squad of guardsmen after her as she raced into the camp; but his main worry was Shimmer. Three solid rows of spearmen slogged through the snow and mud toward us.

"Run," I urged Shimmer.

"It's too late," she answered. I glanced over my shoulder to see a score of spearmen had come up from behind as well.

As the ring of steel closed around us, the Boneless King tried to step forward in the Butcher's body;

but he stumbled as if he were still unused to having real legs. Steadying himself upon a shivering, silk-clad courtier, he declared, "I want the gourd that the girl has. Bring it to me."

When the guard still hesitated, the Boneless King scowled. "Go on. Or I'll have your heads instead of theirs."

But I twirled my staff over my head. "You can take your pick who's going to take your head off." I grinned around me.

"Go on, or I'll have the heads of your families too," the Boneless King threatened. Glancing at one another nervously, the spearmen began to close in. They actually didn't worry me as much as the fifty crossbowmen I could see trotting up.

Things might have gotten a little messy, but right then I heard the distant sound of a jar breaking and a flash of light like lightning. A moment later there was a frightened shout. "Someone's breaking the jars of living fire."

The fire must have spread to the other jars, because the next moment there was a huge roar and a wave of heat rolled through the camp. Steam rose from the suddenly melting snow, and a column of fire soared upward.

"The archives," the chief wizard shouted in alarm

as the fiery tower bellied outward into a ball.

Black, greasy smoke spread through the camp, hiding the tents, and the spearmen halted. For a brief time they were lost from sight, but I could hear them coughing. I hoped that what Civet had said was true: The spell probably worked so long as the Boneless King could see us. But now he was hidden from sight with the rest of the army.

With a spring, I leaped into the air. "Come on, you fat toad," I called to Shimmer. "Let's get out of here before they turn us into pincushions."

Shimmer didn't need a second invitation. "I'd like to see the sewing basket big enough for me." With a flap of her wings, she soared up beside me.

As we flew over the smoke and the shadowy guardsmen, we could see sheets of flame roaring in from the southwest corner of the camp. But big black clouds of smoke hid the actual site of the fire.

Waves of heat rolled toward us as Shimmer banked. Below us, still hidden by the smoke, a half dozen officers were shouting, "Form a bucket brigade. Use snow if you have to."

And at the same time a dozen wizards were shouting, "No, no, water will just make it spread!"

Every now and then there came the sound of shattering pots and a small explosion, as if the last jars were bursting as they heated. But we could see nothing.

Suddenly wizards tumbled out of the cloud of smoke with baskets of blackened scrolls. But the ground had thawed so much that the water turned the soil into a swamp. Up to their ankles in the thick, clinging mud, the wizards looked as if each step were like trying to walk through a vat of glue.

As we circled over the fiery confusion, Thorn called, "Civet!"

Even Shimmer took up the cry: "Civet!" Banking sharply, she flew lower over the camp.

The fire had created a wind that made the tents that were still visible buck and haul at their ropes like wild animals trying to escape. And riding on the wind were sections of burning canvas and silk that landed on the unburned tents. Courtiers, screaming in panic, ran about as they tried to hold their expensive silk robes out of the dirt. Guardsmen stumbled into one another with buckets, pots and even helmets of snow.

"Civet!" we called.

Now the wind seemed to be spreading the fire straight toward us, sending little wings of flame to land on the tops and sides of the tents ahead of us. Cooks staggered out of one huge tent that must have been the kitchen. Between each pair was a large steaming vat. Staggering through the mud, the first pair halted by the entrance where the fire had begun to burn. Leaning back with the vat, they twisted from the waist and lifted the heavy vat upward. Brown stew and onions and chunks of fatty meat flew through the air and onto the fire.

The fire hissed, sending up a tongue of steam to flail at the air, and then it roared even higher and nastier. Onions instantly charred, and cubes of stew meat turned into lumps of charcoal.

Shimmer bravely tried to fly forward, but the oncoming heat rolled over us in waves that even Shimmer felt through her tough hide.

Despite this I could see she was gathering herself up for another try. But I somersaulted in front of her. "No one could live through that."

Shimmer pulled up, and as she hovered, she bowed her head to the flames. "Civet," she said, "your debt is paid."

And then, banking steeply, she flew away over the mountains.

CHAPTER TWENTY-TWO

The children lay flat against Shimmer's back to keep the wind from knocking them off. Overhead, the stars were wheeling across the night sky and the disk of a full moon cast a soft white light over the snowy mountains.

Though Indigo had been full of questions, Thorn uncharacteristically had said nothing. Finally, worried about him, I somersaulted over. "Did you lose your tongue back there?" I asked him.

He seemed to rouse as if from some dream and shook his head. "So it was more than a nightmare. Civet really did have a vision."

Shimmer called over her shoulder, "It was a self-fulfilling prophecy. We make our own destinies."

Thorn chewed his lip as if he would have liked to believe that. "Even so, I wish hers could have been less harsh. She seems to have had nothing but sadness."

Indigo was lying on top of Thorn. "Don't take it that way. I'm sorry she's gone. But she was crazy."

"That's right," Shimmer agreed. "So let's not have anything more about visions." She craned her head around on her long neck to smile at Thorn; but suddenly she stiffened.

Glancing behind us, I saw a speck. I didn't know what bird could be out at night this high up in the mountains; and when we banked, the speck banked as if it were determined to stay with us.

Reluctantly I came to the only conclusion I could. "That dragon's following us."

Shimmer swung her head forward. "Pomfret's been getting fat in the Butcher's palace. He can't keep up with me."

"Pomfret?" I asked.

"My brother." Shimmer grimaced as if the words left a bad taste in her mouth. "It's bad enough that he abandoned our people in the dragon kingdoms; but now he's betraying our entire race."

I wasn't as confident that Shimmer could win the race. He might have been the Butcher's spoiled pet; but Shimmer had been trapped in a mountain and kicked around from sea to mountain. However, I knew better than to say anything, instead contenting myself with merely following Shimmer as she banked down a valley. The wind whipped the snow up from the ridges like a ghostly army—as if the Boneless King's ancient kingdom were awakening once again.

Shimmer cut through a cleft in the ridge top where the rock lay in folds and ripples like frozen curtains. And then, her breath rising in steamy plumes from the sides of her mouth, she banked sharply to the right.

Hovering for a moment, I risked a look behind us. Shimmer's brother was even closer than before. Straining my eyes in the moonlight, I could make out two flealike objects on Pomfret's back. Skipping through the air, I rejoined Shimmer. "I think the Boneless King is with him."

The altitude and the cold quickly began to take their toll on us. My own sides were heaving like a set of bellows; and beside me Shimmer was already panting, her sides laboring as she beat her wings rapidly in the thin air. And the moisture in my own breath froze as soon as it left my mouth, forming an icy beard on my chin. We both began losing altitude until we were almost skimming over the mountains. With difficulty, Shimmer twisted her head around and swore. "That little worm is gaining."

"The Boneless King is probably using his magic to keep him warm," I gasped. I took another one of my usual leaps; but instead of feeling the air as solid as a floor, my paws couldn't find any support. To my shock, I felt myself falling.

Next to me, Shimmer was plummeting through the air as well. "The Boneless King must be close enough to cast his flightless spell again." And with one last, great effort, she turned herself so that her own body would cushion the landing for the children.

Whether it was the Boneless King's intention or not, we landed in a huge snowdrift. It was like sinking into a deep—if chilly—pillow. Blinking the snow from my eyes, I began to crawl up out of the hole just as Pomfret spiraled down to the snowy surface. On his back were the Boneless King and Horn, the little wizard he used to disguise his own magic. I suppose the Boneless King had taken him along to fool the people back in camp.

"I really must thank you," the Boneless King said, smiling. "I haven't had so much fun in a long time."

As Shimmer rose, spluttering, from the snow, Pomfret recognized his sister instantly. Lifting his head in astonishment, he almost unseated his passengers. "You! I thought you were dead."

Shimmer crawled onto the surface, the snow crunching under her belly. "Thought or wished?"

But the Boneless King didn't care a fig about family reunions. "Now let's see what's so important about that gourd," he said, and tapped the back of the little wizard's head. Instantly, Horn's hands flew up, but of course it was the Boneless King who actually worked the magic.

And even if Shimmer or I had known the spell to block him, I don't think we could have worked it quickly enough. Indigo had put her arms protectively around the gourd; but in the blink of an eye it had changed into the cauldron.

The Boneless King leaned forward. "No, that couldn't be . . ." Suddenly he smiled in breathless delight. "But it is." Then he saw the crack. "Only it's broken."

Pomfret also recognized one of the great treasures of the dragons. "How did you get Uncle Sambar to give that to you?"

"I . . . unh . . . borrowed it so I could restore our people's home." Shimmer reared her head up to appeal to her brother. "You were their king once. Help us."

"And still am king," Pomfret insisted.

The Boneless King kicked the back of Pomfret's neck with his heel. "Since you know this dragon, you might as well take the cauldron from her."

Pomfret, though, stayed put. "I only said I'd help fly you."

The Boneless King kicked Pomfret again. "You like that little magical treasure of mine." He lowered his voice menacingly. "Well, it can be destroyed."

"You wouldn't," Pomfret gasped.

"Don't tell me what I choose to do." The Boneless King slid from Pomfret's back, and Horn followed reluctantly. "It won't do any good to use your tail hairs either," he called to me. "My wonderful friend here will see to that." And he slapped Horn's back.

The wizard bowed uncertainly as if he were still not sure how he was working his magic.

As Pomfret took a step forward, Shimmer scowled. "It's bad enough being a pet, but letting him set you against your own flesh and blood—that's outrageous."

Pomfret dipped his head unhappily. "You don't understand. I have to."

"I'll take the king," I whispered to Shimmer. "You take on your brother." But as Thorn reached for his dagger, I shook my head. "And you and Indigo run for all you're worth."

"No," Thorn objected stubbornly.

"The world still has to be warned," I insisted.

"And the cauldron must be kept from his hands," Shimmer added.

"Why do you have to prolong the inevitable?" the king wondered affably. "You know you can't win. Surrender."

"We're going to die anyway." Shimmer stamped her feet in the snow to get some purchase. "We know too much."

"But the question is the speed. You may die either quickly or . . ." The Boneless King broke off as the sky suddenly began to redden, and he looked up just as puzzled as the rest of us.

"It's not his magic," I whispered to Thorn.

The dark valley steadily filled with the red light until it was as bright as a sunrise. But though the Boneless King had stopped his own spell casting, Horn tried to work his own magic. With horrible scowls and frenetic waves of his hands, he cast a spell.

I was ready for the ground to open beneath us, for monsters to pop out of nowhere—for most anything, in fact, except for the three giant bubbles that suddenly appeared and whirled right over us.

When they popped, I could smell the soapy film now clinging to my fur. "What kind of magic is this?"

Horn clutched his hands miserably in front of him. "I provide entertainment at banquets. But for a little while I was a great wizard."

Pivoting in the snow, the Boneless King vaulted onto Pomfret's back. "Fly," he ordered.

Pomfret, though, was still distracted by the increasing light. "I—"

"Fly, you fool." And the Boneless King kicked at Pomfret's sides.

"No, don't leave me." Horn ran toward the dragon.

Lifting his foot, the Boneless King set his boot against the little wizard's face and sent him tumbling backward into the snow. "Fly," the Boneless King ordered.

Dazed, Pomfret spread his wings.

"Your Highness, wait for me." Horn floundered through the snow until he was standing up.

"Fly!"

As Pomfret began to rise in the air, Horn threw himself at the dragon's tail. "Don't abandon me." And he wrapped his arms and legs around Pomfret's tail as tightly as a drowning man clinging to a log.

The dragon bucked in the air at the unexpected

weight, and for a moment I thought he was going to dump his two riders back onto the snow; but somehow Pomfret managed to right himself and flew out of sight.

As the valley glowed with the strange red light, I gave a whoop. "We can relax now. We're safe."

Shimmer stared at a dark shadow that appeared on the snow. The black circle began to spread outward until it filled almost the entire valley. "How do you figure that?"

As pebbles and soil began to patter down in a gentle shower, Indigo crouched. "Ow." She and Thorn pressed themselves against the dragon, who raised a wing protectively.

I took the opportunity to join them in their shelter. "It's bright as a sunrise even if it is night." And I was feeling so good that I couldn't help laughing.

Shimmer had twisted her long neck, so her head was tucked under her wing like a bird's. "Will you tell me what's happening?"

"Did you send the signal?" I asked.

"Well, yes," she said.

I tweaked her snout. "Then it got through to the Smith and the Snail Woman. Their mountain is coming."

CHAPTER TWENTY-THREE

The dirt and pebbles made a steady patter on Shimmer's outstretched wing as we peered out from underneath it. At first I could see the silhouette of a mountain about a hundred meters above our head.

About five hundred meters in diameter at its base, it rose some three hundred meters more to a peak, and its sides were covered with hundreds of spikes that made it look like some pincushion. But some of the spikes ended in hollow loops, and looked more like giant needles, while others corkscrewed at odd angles like sad dough sticks. Some of them had fused together to form intricate webs, and still others were like giant, crumbling melons full of holes.

"See those funny shapes on the sides?" I pointed at a cluster of treelike shapes that bristled around the base. "They say that those are thieves. It might be wise to be on your good behavior."

Shimmer twisted her head around to glare at me. "You're the one who ought to have that advice tattooed on your head. *I* always took high marks in etiquette."

I mugged at her. "Who else was in your class? Eels and oysters?"

All this time the top of the silhouette had been edged in red light. But as the mountain solidified, the top began to glow and shoot off sparks. "Is it a volcano?" Thorn asked.

I ducked away from a sooty pebble. "It's the fires of their forge."

The blackness overhead began to solidify into chunks of different kinds of rock. There was gray granite, darkish-blue slabs of slate, hunks of streaked marble and so on—and all of them welded together by veins of gold. "They," I went on to explain, "are what's left over after the war when the Serpent Lady finished repairing the crack in the sky that the Boneless King caused."

When the mountain had finished materializing, the rain of dirt stopped and a purple object shot from the side of the mountain into the air. As it swung down toward us, I could see that it was a bronze chariot pulled by huge cranes of the same material. Purple vapor rose from the spinning wheels like clouds of dust.

Riding in the chariot was a woman who seemed to have a hunched back under a cloak of yellow satin; but when the wind of her passage made her cloak billow out behind her, we could see that she had a giant shell like a snail's. But this shell was all silvery, with iridescent colors following its spirals.

Thorn gasped, but I motioned for him to be quiet. "That's the Snail Woman, the Smith's wife."

There were no reins visible—rather she guided her birds with gestures from a folded fan and brought her chariot to a smooth landing on the snow. As it rolled to a stop, I noticed that despite the chariot's weight, the wheels left no tracks.

The Snail Woman's silvery hair had been done up into braids and curled on the sides of her head to match the spiraling pattern of her shell. Her eyes were small and her cheeks broad, making her eyes seem even smaller; and yet there was a pleasant twinkle to them. "Are you the ones who called us?"

Shimmer lifted her head up and folded in her wing, trying to straighten up with all the dignity she could muster. "Yes."

"There's the smell of resin still to you." She chuckled and studied Shimmer. "It's been a long time since a dragon sent a summons—or anyone, for that matter." Her eyes examined the cliffs. "When I last saw these mountains, they were new with sharp edges. Now they're all worn down. Has it really been that long?"

"Much has happened in the world," Shimmer said, "and not all of it good."

The Snail Woman beamed at Indigo and Thorn. "Are these your pets?"

"Companions, lady," Shimmer corrected her before they could say anything.

"Either way, they need a washing badly." She cocked her head to the left and then to the right. "And who's that hiding behind the children? Come on out where I can see you."

I had thought it politic to scrunch down until I could see what her mood was like. I stepped out now and gave a deep bow. "Hello, my lady."

She drew her eyebrows together with a frown. "No. It couldn't be. I assumed that you had been hanged a long time ago."

Shimmer glanced down at me. "But you know his master, the Old Boy," she said, repeating my own words to her.

The Snail Woman tapped her folded fan against her palm. "True, but I also know this rascal."

I dragged my foot in the snow. "Forgive and forget, my lady."

She continued to tap her fan impatiently against her palm. "You snuck into our mountain where it floated between the worlds and tried to steal my fan."

I took off my cap contritely. "I had need, my lady. There was a whole mountain on fire."

"That you set to flame in the first place." Though it was still cold and snowy, the woman flapped her fan open. It was all of iron and decorated with cranes dancing beside a pond where fish leaped.

People are always misunderstanding me. "Anyway, my master, the Old Boy, has made me pay for my crimes. I've been doing nothing but good deeds since."

"And probably committed a new crime for every old crime absolved." The Snail Woman flicked her wrist, and a wind suddenly blew snow up into all our faces. "Well, birds of a feather flock together." And she raised her fan as if she were going to blow us from the Desolate Mountains.

Hurriedly, I threw myself face forward in the snow. "Please, my lady, the Nameless One now has a form and a name and is loose in the mountains."

The Snail Woman sucked in her breath sharply. "This is ill news. We must find him, and quickly. What form has he taken?"

Despite a mouthful of snow, I didn't dare to look up. "The king of this land. He calls himself The Butcher, but everyone else thinks of him as the ruler."

"Worse and worse. But"—she paused suspiciously—"you seem to know a good deal about this. If this was your doing, it was shamefully done."

Thorn copied me and threw himself in the snow beside me. "Don't blame him, my lady. It was all my fault."

"Will you stop that?" Shimmer said in exasperation. "You couldn't have foreseen it. We just wanted to get off the island. And if there's anyone to blame, it's all of us."

"Enough." Snapping her fan shut with a click, the Snail Woman tapped first me and then Thorn. "My husband must hear the tale as well, so you'd best rise and come with me."

I rose to my knees, dusting off the snow, and helped Thorn to his feet. When the children had clambered onto Shimmer's back, the woman pointed her fan at the cranes, and with a squeak they spread their wings and then, with loud creaks, began to flap them. As the cranes rose into the air, they pulled the chariot up behind them. As Shimmer flew after her, the Snail Woman turned slowly in the air. "And my invitation is especially for you, my fine Monkey."

Under the threat of her fan, I somersaulted after them. "I . . . unh . . . didn't want to interrupt your husband's work. But it's always . . . unh . . . such a pleasure to chat with him."

"I think you know the way," the woman said; and leaving twin plumes of purple vapor, she glided in behind me.

With a yelp, I barely got my tail out of the way of a crane's clashing beak. With the cranes giving me "encouragement" with their beaks, I cartwheeled up toward her home.

As I drew closer, I could see the sparks flying from the mountaintop and illuminating the strange peaks along its sides. Here and there a cave glowed red as if opened on the forge. Petrified pine trees, their trunks twisted in odd shapes, grew all around the base.

I headed straight for a huge cave, and Shimmer followed. I motioned her over to the side just in time as the Snail Woman landed smoothly. As soon as the chariot stopped, the harness rose and folded back into the chariot while the cranes stepped away.

Thorn couldn't help gaping at the mechanical birds. "How do those creatures fly? They're amazing."

The Snail Woman seemed pleased by his reaction. "You know, it's been so long ago that I don't remember. My husband and I put them together out of scrap; but they've given us far more pleasure than any other creation of our forge." Then, pointing her fan at the mouth of the cave, she commanded the cranes, "Go out and patrol."

Spreading their wings with an obedient creak, the cranes flew out. I could see them begin to circle around the mountain. As I watched them alertly, the Snail Woman tapped me upon the head. "Just don't get any idea of helping yourself to any of our treasures."

"I wouldn't think of it, my lady," I murmured, and bowed.

"Not if you'll get caught, I daresay." And she pointed her fan at a tunnel. "That way."

The tunnel corkscrewed up and away from the cave and into another chamber piled with mounds of various types and colors of ore. Under her watchful eye we were led from cave to cave—some filled with more ore, others with strange machines and creations—until we came to a large cavern. Against one wall were shelves covered with scrolls. And on the table burned several braziers where pots boiled and bubbled.

At the table was a thin man in a cloak like the woman's. But his exposed arms and legs were so bony that he seemed to be all angles. One ear protruded from the side of his head with a forward slant, while the other ear had a backward slant. And even his nose was sharp and crooked. One spindly leg was shorter than the other.

"Is that the Smith?" Thorn whispered to me. "I don't see how he can work the forge with those thin arms."

As we entered, he was just pouring a silver liquid from a jar into a copper pot; and there was an immediate flash of brilliant blue light that soared in a column to smash against the roof and curve outward.

"Blast," he grumbled with a wriggle of his ears. "I've burned our lunch."

"Dear," the Snail Woman said, "I've brought visitors."

"I hope they're not hungry." The Smith turned and scowled ferociously when he saw me. "You! Haven't you caused enough trouble?"

His expression was so merciless that I gave up all hope of gaining any help from him. Giving several quick bows, I started to back toward the entrance. "Yes, I have. And so if you'll excuse me, I'll take my leave."

But the Snail Woman had been prepared for just

such a maneuver and poked her folded fan into my back. "Wait," she commanded me. And then to her husband, she explained, "They've helped the Nameless One to escape."

The Smith was so irritated that his ears threatened to flap away from his head. "Impossible. My grandmother and the other masters worked out their curse very thoroughly. It took years to work out the details."

"And they say he has a shape and a name." The Snail Woman gave me a poke. "What did you say it was?"

I squirmed. "The Boneless King."

"Inconceivable." The angry Smith had seized a wriggling ear in either hand.

"And he is now posing as the ruler of the land." The Snail Woman lifted her fan away.

"Unbelievable." Still holding on to his ears, the Smith limped over to a stool and plopped down, crushing the pile of scrolls that lay on it. Sitting down, he was even more angular than standing up. He looked glumly at the copper pot. "Well, I couldn't have eaten lunch anyway after that news. You'd better tell us how all this happened."

Shimmer explained the events, and when she finished she glanced at me. "And if the fault is anyone's it's mine. It was I who decided to bring the cauldron to you to fix."

"No," Thorn insisted, "it's my fault."

The Smith cautiously lifted a hand away from one ear. Reassured that it was now still, he freed his other ear. "Let me see the cauldron."

At a nod from Shimmer, Indigo slipped the cauldron from around her neck and set it before the Smith.

Almost immediately, he swept it up with a crow of delight. "I recognize this. It was one of the last of my grandmother's creations and served her well in the war. Look at the superb craftsmanship. This was the greatest of the Serpent Lady's masterpieces." He began to turn it around in his hands lovingly, but stopped when he saw the crack.

The Smith clucked his tongue sadly. "Tsk, tsk, tsk, that's a pity."

Shimmer rubbed her throat nervously. "Can't you fix it?"

The Smith held the cauldron up in one hand while he pointed at it with the other. "It's more a question of healing than fixing. My grandmother worked in the old magic. They all did in those days. But then folk began to question the rightness of such magic.

And that was why the Great War was fought." He set it down. "What was created with the old magic must be fixed with the old magic. And that I cannot and will not do."

Shimmer stepped forward eagerly. "But with this I could give a home to my people—a home they desperately need."

The Smith set the cauldron on his lap. "Even if I were willing, would you pay the price?"

Shimmer raised a paw. "Anything," she swore.

The Snail Woman crossed the room to examine the cauldron herself. "Never offer that answer until you know what the price may be."

Shimmer held out both paws to indicate the cauldron. "It means a home for my people. Someone has already given her life."

His hands resting on the sides of the cauldron, the Smith looked at each of us in turn. "And the price would not end there. It might require a soul—a human soul. After the war, it was agreed that even the methods of the old magic should be kept secret so that others could not revive it. But this"—he tapped the cauldron—"was created before the great oath. And that meant someone was sacrificed to give power to this cauldron. In essence, the power comes from the soul that now dwells within the metal."

Shimmer reared up in horror. "There's someone trapped inside?"

The Smith nodded his head solemnly. "In effect."

Shimmer gazed at the cauldron and then looked back at the Smith. "Perhaps it could be fixed—I mean, healed—without the old magic."

The Smith tugged thoughtfully at one ear. "It's true that my wife and I have learned much over the aeons."

"We should be considering the real threat of the Nameless One," the Snail Woman said, "rather than debating abstract problems in theoretical magic."

The Smith stood up as if his mind was made up. "I think best when I'm at the forge." He cradled the cauldron in his arms as if it were a baby. "The answer will come to me after we try to fix it."

They looked silently at one another for a moment; and then his wife nodded as if they had reached some understanding. "So be it," she said.

CHAPTER TWENTY-FOUR

The forge was a large, airy room, open at the top so that we could see the moon and stars faintly up above. Thorn whispered to me, "I was expecting something dim and smelly."

With his big ears the Smith overheard him and waved his hand around grandly. "Do you think artists can create in dim, smelly rooms? Our magic keeps the heat in but also lets in the light during the daytime."

At the moment, though, the red light was coming from the circular hearth in the center of the room. The walls, floor and ceiling, which were already red and slick as glass, seemed almost a blood red; but within the glass were little specks of gold. Nor were the walls flat, but more like layers of cake batter that had been poured down the sides and over the bottom of a box.

And etched within the smooth material of the walls were the giant outlines of tigers and dragons.

The Smith saw where Thorn and I were gazing and explained, "Tigers are the symbol of fire, dragons the symbol of metal."

Mounted on a column of the same red material as the wall was a large iron anvil with a spur at either end; and laid out on a table and a rear wall were various blacksmithing tools. There were tongs, hammers, clamps, files, shears and tonglike things that the Smith said were scrapers to smooth out the sides of something he was creating.

The central hearth was about two meters in diameter, formed of black stones fitted together without any mortar that I could see. On each stone were pictures in the same picture writing as in the crypt under the lake; and in the center of the hearth were the oddest coals I had ever seen—like coiled snakes. Their softly glowing bodies filled the room and air well with a lurid red light. It was the hearth that made the mountain glow like a volcano and made the night sky as bright as sunrise.

"So this is where you forged my staff," I said, peering over the side.

"As a present for the King of the Golden Sea," the Snail Woman corrected me. She was shadowing me as if she were convinced I had come to borrow something else from their forge.

"Why are people always misinterpreting what I do?" I complained. "It wasn't like that old dragon was using it. Something that's made so nicely is meant to be seen and admired."

The Snail Woman smiled cynically. "Like my fan?"

"I'm reformed now." Over the coals hung a long metal box from which a handle stuck out at one end. Curious, I grabbed the handle and shoved it in. Immediately air wheezed out from a hole in the bottom of the box. "What is it?"

"A box bellows," the Smith said as he shed his cloak. "The handle shoves a sheet of metal back and forth inside the box, driving air out through the hole on the bottom. That way air comes out when you push at the handle *and* when you pull." He was wearing only a kind of kilt, and I could see that his arms and legs, though skinny, were roped with muscle.

The Snail Woman made a sign over the hearth, and the coals began to brighten to a ruby red as if they were catching on fire. "Since you're so curious about the bellows, you can work the handle."

I shoved the handle back and forth in a slow, steady rhythm. "Like this?"

"A little faster." The Snail Woman put her hand

on my wrist and guided me for a moment until I worked the bellows at the pace she wanted.

"You can put the cauldron on the coals." When the Smith turned to hang up his cloak on a peg, I could see his back was covered with green moss.

Not wanting to stare at him, I watched as Shimmer set the cauldron on the hearth. "Here?" she asked.

Over his head he slipped a long gown that looked as if it were made of white wool. "A meter to the right," he said, and when Shimmer obeyed, he nodded. "That's fine."

"No, that gown's dirty, dear." Now that I was occupied at the bellows, the Snail Woman thought it was safe to go over to her husband. "How many times do I have to tell you not to wear a dirty gown? You look like a beggar." Handing her husband another gown, she took the stained one and threw it on the floor.

As the Smith helped his wife into a gown of her own, I watched the coals in the forge, which were now pulsing a scarlet red. I decided that they must be magical too, because they grew hot so fast. Suddenly the coal began to uncoil. I couldn't help yelping in fright. "It's alive."

Within the hot hearth, a glowing rat stared back

at me for a moment and then began crawling over the other coals.

"Don't worry." The Smith chuckled. "The fire-rats won't bite you. But you should be in a gown anyway. Sometimes one of them gets excited and climbs out; and you won't like it much when they cuddle up to you."

"When?" I gulped and headed hastily over to the wall, where more gowns hung. They all seemed to be the same large size, so they hung on Indigo, Thorn and me like tents. Fortunately, there were ropes of the same material with which we could cinch our clothes up. Indigo began to scratch immediately. "It's kind of itchy."

"Better to scratch than to burn. It's made from their wool." The Snail Woman indicated the fire-rats in the hearth with her fan and then tucked it away inside her sleeve. As the first creature crept about, its fur began to brush out into a bushy, glowing coat, making it look more like a hedgehog now.

"Botheration," Shimmer grumbled as she struggled to cram her large body into a gown.

The Smith selected a pair of long iron tongs. "You could shrink a bit."

Before Shimmer could answer, I raised my nose

haughtily and mimicked her. "A dragon princess must be a dragonish size."

It seemed that the Smith had had dealings with dragons before, because he merely shrugged. "Well, it's your hide that will burn. Our little pets get pretty excited once they're awake."

So when Shimmer joined me at the bellows, I noticed that she was of a smaller size and the gown protected all of her. Together, we began to slide the handle back and forth rapidly.

The Smith picked up the cauldron with the tongs as easily as if it were only a feather and set it in the middle of the hearth. "Wake up, children. See the new toy our guests have brought for you.

"Wake up, wake up," he called, waving his tongs as if it were a conductor's baton. At his command a dozen more coils uncurled into the shape of little rats. The next instant they were leaping about on top of one another as if playing a game of tag. "Fun's fun, but it's time to rouse the others." And the Smith clicked the tongs open and shut. Obediently, the conscious fire-rats began to nudge the others to life.

As more of the fire-rats began to stir and move about, the Snail Woman got another pair of tongs and picked up the soiled gown from the floor, where she had dropped it.

The Smith frowned at her in annoyance. "Do you have to do the laundry now?"

"You can show off all you like when the laundry's finished," she announced calmly, and set the gown within the hearth. Immediately, some of the fire-rats began to wriggle over it, licking at the stains. Little tongues of blue flames instantly spurted up and died down, and I waited for the gown to burn. But when the Snail Woman lifted the gown out once again, I could see that it was pure and white as if all the stains had been burned away.

While his pragmatic wife hung their laundry back up, the Smith clinked his tongs against the side of the cauldron. "Come, my sweet ones. Time to play."

The clinking of the tongs drew the fire-rats to the cauldron, and they began climbing up the sides and leaping into the cauldron itself. Soon scarlet sheets of flame burst into life, rising up into the air to dissipate. All the time, the Smith used his tongs to tease the slower fire-rats to join their mates around the cauldron.

In the meantime, the Snail Woman had selected a pair of medium-sized hammers, which she held in either hand. "Ready."

But the Smith wigwagged his ears back and forth.

[275]

"A moment more." He waited for a long count and then gently eased his tongs between squirming bodies to grasp the cauldron itself. Lifting it into the air, he turned it upside down and shook out his remaining pets.

There was a ringing sound as he set it over one of the anvil's spurs so that the crack was facing upward. The whole cauldron now glowed a bronze red. Indigo edged in curiously. "Except for the crack, it looks like it's new."

"The green patina came from aging. And it leaves with the years as the cauldron heals." He eyed his wife, who had him shift the cauldron around slightly.

"Keep the fire-rats awake," the Snail Woman ordered us without looking over.

We kept pumping obediently, and the Snail Woman lifted her right hand above her head and brought it down on the cauldron with a loud clank. As the hammer bounced up again, she brought down the hammer in her left hand. While her husband held the cauldron on the anvil itself, she beat a steady kind of metallic music until the perspiration made her hair cling to her forehead.

Finally she rested her hammers on her shoulders. The crack in the cauldron hadn't narrowed one bit.

"You were right," she observed to her husband. "It wasn't hot enough."

"All of you get on the bellows," the Smith ordered, and easing the cauldron from the anvil, he set it back in the hearth again.

Indigo and Thorn squeezed in with Shimmer and me; and the four of us began working the handle until the box bellows rocked back and forth. As gusts of air blew from it over the hearth, the Smith kept urging his pets to scamper over the cauldron. "Play, children. Play. Rub it, scrub it."

Inside the stones, the fire-rats kept getting more and more excited, and they began skipping about or whirling in circles as they tried to catch their tails. And they changed from a ruddy glow to a bright golden color. Suddenly one of them leaped out of the hearth and began racing around and around the room, its little claws clicking on the smooth floor. I was glad, then, that I had the fire-proof gown on.

With a well-practiced dip, the Smith caught the fire-rat with his tongs and lifted it gently back into the hearth. "I don't think we can get it hot enough. You'd better give us a hand."

Setting down the hammers on the table, the Snail

Woman slipped her fan from her sleeve. "I might melt it."

"My grandmother didn't make silly little kitchen pots." The Smith jerked his head for her to come over to the hearth.

Snapping her fan open, the Snail Woman flicked her wrist ever so slightly; and the resulting wind from her fan was enough to knock Thorn, Indigo and me against Shimmer. We all stayed still as flames rolled in a column straight up the light well; and the fire-rats swelled to the size of cats.

And now, as the rats began to leap about, they were so large that they knocked the cauldron this way and that. In fact, the Smith had to hold the cauldron steady with his tongs.

"Get back to the bellows," the Snail Woman barked at us as she put the fan away.

We leaped back to the handle and pumped faster and faster while the Snail Woman and the Smith studied the cauldron critically.

"Now," she said.

The Smith wriggled his ears in annoyance. "I still don't think it's ready."

"And I say take it out now." The Snail Woman was already returning to the anvil.

With his tongs the Smith again lifted the cauldron

[*278*]

from the hearth and shook off his pets. Setting it over the anvil, he held it for his wife, who had once again picked up her hammers.

This time the Snail Woman brought her hammer down in a blow that would have knocked out Shimmer. The moment her hammer struck the cauldron's side, it rang like a giant bell, filling the whole room with its melodic vibrations until my teeth shivered and I felt as if I were inside a giant bell itself.

And with a joyful cry, a green light fountained upward from the cauldron, fusing into a solid ball that raced around and around the room.

"Oh, no," the Smith moaned.

But even as he spoke, the ball of light found the opening in the ceiling and shot upward through the air well to disappear in the sky itself. Whatever magic kept the heat in could not keep the ball of light from escaping.

Immediately Shimmer let go of the bellows handle. "What's wrong?" she asked.

The Snail Woman lowered her hammers. "I suppose we should be happy for the poor creature inside."

The Smith's shoulders sagged. "But the magic's undone now. And we may be undone as well."

I clung to the bellows handle. "What happened?"

The Smith lifted the cauldron off the anvil and stared at it sorrowfully. "The soul that was imprisoned within the cauldron is now free. And without the soul, there is nothing on which the magic can draw."

Shimmer came around the hearth. "Perhaps if the crack were fixed anyway?"

"It's beyond healing." He shook the cauldron at her. "It's just an antique now."

But if there's one thing a dragon can do well, it's be stubborn. "We've come so far and risked so much, won't you try one more time?"

"It won't do any good," the Smith insisted.

The Snail Woman laid her hammers down on the table with loud clinks and drew her fan from her sleeve. "We ought to try."

With a shrug, the Smith returned the cauldron to the hearth. "If you're willing, then so am I."

Determined to mend the cauldron, we took up our positions again at the bellows while the Snail Woman got ready with her fan. But this time when the Smith clinked his tongs against the cauldron, he urged, "Attack, children. Attack."

As the fire-rats began to swarm over the cauldron, we began shoving and pulling at the handle as fast as we could. At the same time, the Snail Woman flicked her fan in carefully controlled bursts of wind.

Within the hearth the fire-rats ballooned to the size of small dogs, until the hearth walls barely seemed high enough to contain them; and the Smith was forced to use his tongs to hold his pets within the stones.

Gusts of yellow flame soared steadily from the hearth, making the sky above the mountain glow as bright as day. Thorn, Indigo and I were all sweating inside our woolen gowns; and their damp gowns clung to the bodies of the Smith and the Snail Woman. And yet each time the Snail Woman asked him, the Smith would judge the cauldron with a critical eye and then declare that it still wasn't hot enough.

Finally, when the walls themselves began to melt and large glasslike drops began to ooze down, the Snail Woman put her fan away. "Let's try it now," she said.

"All right, but it's still not ready." Lifting the cauldron from the hearth, the Smith quickly set it over the anvil. And he was right. Pound as hard and as skillfully as she could, the Snail Woman could not fix the crack.

Shimmer slumped down on the floor. "I've failed my people."

"We may have failed the world." The Smith's ears drooped gloomily. "Of the Five Masters, the dragon,

Calambac, has gone on; and so have my grandmother and the Archer. I must find the Unicorn. If I can't, we could all be in a great deal of trouble."

"There's the Lord of the Flowers," I suggested.

The Smith shook his head. "I'll try, but he has wearied of the world, and may not help—even against his old enemy."

"And then there's my master, the Old Boy," I suggested. "He went voyaging somewhere among the worlds."

He looked at me sharply. "If you don't know where your master is, how do you expect me to find him?"

I shrugged. "Look for him at the same time you search for the Unicorn."

"I'll try," the Smith said, sighing, "but we alone may have to oppose the will of the Boneless King."

Thorn looked around at our discouraged faces for a moment, and then he tried to speak; but his parched throat would only let him croak. "Do you think that the cauldron could stop the Nameless One?" He remembered to use the old name for the Boneless King.

The Smith ran his tongs along the cauldron's crack. "It helped once before. Floods swept away his armies and stunned him so he could be captured."

Thorn stood, lost in thought, while the rest of us

tried to get back our wind in that hot forge. Finally he went over to the Smith and plucked at his now-blackened sleeve. "Will you try again?"

The Smith let his tongs dangle down. "What's the use, boy?"

Thorn tried to lick his dried lips, but there didn't seem to be enough moisture in his mouth for even that. "Did your grandmother always give up so easily?" he asked slyly.

"No, but my grandmother was not always wise," the Smith said.

But the Snail Woman used a hammer to guide the Smith's tongs back to the cauldron. "I say the boy's right. Let's try one last time."

I tried to raise an arm and found that I couldn't. "I ache in every muscle."

Shimmer eyed me with a pretended glee. "Don't tell me that a dragon's outlasted you."

"I can outlast twelve dragons," I groaned as I shuffled back to the bellows. "But I wish that I didn't have to."

"This is stupid," Indigo said to Thorn; but she took her place beside me anyway.

As Thorn squeezed in beside Shimmer once again, he looked as if he wanted to say something urgent to her. "Shimmer—" he began.

But by that time the Smith had swung the cauldron back inside the hearth, and the Snail Woman had begun fanning their pets once more.

"Attack, children, attack," the Smith urged his pets.

"Wait a moment," Shimmer called, and looked questioningly at Thorn. However, by then he was so busy working the bellows that he didn't have the wind to speak.

Through our combined efforts, the fire-rats swelled to the size of large dogs thudding against the black stones. Voice hoarse with the effort, the Smith kept urging on his pets as the flames rolled steadily upward, brilliant as the sun.

I kept thinking this time that the cauldron would get hot enough. But each time his wife asked him, the Smith would give an irritated wriggle of his ears.

Finally, he used his tongs to prod his pets away from the cauldron. "It's no use. We're the ones who are going to melt before this cauldron becomes soft enough."

CHAPTER TWENTY-FIVE

When I heard the Smith say those words, I looked at Shimmer. But she was slumping like a beaten dog even as she went on working the bellows, and so were Indigo and Monkey.

All the while we had been working, I had thought over what the others had said. Perhaps it really wasn't my fault. Perhaps it wasn't anyone's fault. Assigning the blame wasn't the important thing. Stopping the Boneless King was. I had seen the wastelands he had created and heard his promise to do the same to the entire world. And even from our brief contact with him, I knew how cruel and relentless he could be. Not only did he have his old magic now, but he had the Butcher's army and an entire kingdom to follow him.

And this time there was no one to stop him.

Except for me. None of them could see what had to be

done to fix the cauldron—when it was as plain as the snout on Shimmer's face.

Civet had said I would know when it was my time. And the moment I acknowledged that fact, I suddenly felt a kind of peace inside—as if I were connected to something bigger and stronger than me. I was still a little scared, but also felt as if I were part of something powerful— something flowing on to a destination for which it was meant. And that helped ease my fears a little bit. Shimmer would have back her sea, and then the Smith would have his weapon against the Boneless King.

Letting go of the handle, I straightened up.

"Don't stop now, Thorn," Indigo scolded me.

I ignored her. "It's my time," I tried to explain, but the words caught in my throat as the flames towered over my head. Before I lost my nerve, I grasped the stones of the wall. They were hot to the touch, but I didn't let myself snatch my hands away. Instead, I hauled myself up to the top. Before me the huge fire-rats were scuttling about.

"Thorn," Shimmer cried from behind me, "get down from there."

I wanted to say good-bye to her, but the heat was so scorching that no words would come. I could only look at my battered old dragon one last time.

She had let go of the bellows. "This is no time to be playing games," she snapped, and started to reach for me.

I couldn't let her pull me back. Facing the hearth and my destiny, I leaped upon the cauldron.

As I pressed myself against the hot metal sides, the fire-rats tumbled against me. I thought they were going to attack me as they had the cauldron; but apparently it was different with people. They were as curious and eager to play as puppies; and as they brushed up against me in greeting, a yellow wall of flames rose up all around and shut out the world. And for a moment, despite the gown, I felt a pain so intense that I could not describe it.

"No-o-o-o!" Shimmer's agonized cry seemed to come from far, far away. And the others' voices seemed to come from a great distance as well.

But the pain was gone as suddenly as it had come. I felt as if the dirt were burning away from my body just as it had from the Smith's gown. And more than my body. It was as if the impurities were burning away from my soul. I could see how petty my jealousy of Indigo had been.

And knowing that made me feel as free as the moon above.

Suddenly I felt an urge to stretch out my arms and embrace the glowing white sphere, but my arms would not move. They seemed fused to my sides; and my body itself began to harden, harder than flesh, harder than Shimmer's armored hide.

And I knew I was as hard as the dragon cauldron.

And the next instant it was as if I had eyes on each side of me as well as behind, because I could see a full three hundred sixty degrees. Shimmer, still weeping, was trying to reach through the flames, and Monkey, Indigo and the Smith were struggling to hold her back.

I tried to tell them that I was all right, but they couldn't hear me.

Only the Snail Woman had the presence of mind to get ready with her fan once again. "He's not gone," she said to all of them. "He's in the cauldron now. And with his help we might heal it after all."

CHAPTER TWENTY-SIX

When Thorn jumped into the hearth, Shimmer would have followed him. "No-o-o-o!" she cried. Instantly, I threw myself in front of her.

"Thorn is gone," I said to her.

"Let go of me, you fool ape," she snapped at me.

Indigo started shoving at the dragon's other shoulder. "No one could survive in that heat."

Shimmer brushed the girl aside with a forepaw, and her tail easily swatted me away, knocking us both to the floor.

The Smith was tugging at his ears in horror; but as he felt the dragon move toward the hearth, he seemed to wake from a terrible nightmare. "You can't help the boy now," he said, and bringing up his arm, he caught Shimmer across the chest. I had never met anyone able to match a dragon's strength until that moment. I guess centuries of working at the forge had given the Smith incredible muscles. Shimmer seemed to be shoving against a solid steel bar. The next moment Indigo and I had sprung to our feet and were helping him.

But right at that moment the Snail Woman turned to us calmly. "He's not gone," she insisted. "He's in the cauldron now. And with his help we might heal it after all."

However, despite all her efforts to obtain the cauldron, Shimmer had no heart for it now. "It would be tainted."

The Smith lowered his arm and looked at his wife. "And we have sworn against using such magic."

The Snail Woman glared at her husband and the dragon as if they were the biggest fools. "There is no evil in this magic. He did it of his own free will. Would you have his sacrifice be for nothing?"

Indigo let go of Shimmer. "That doesn't seem right either. If anyone should have sacrificed a life, it was me—not him," Shimmer moaned. Her head drooped and the tears welled in her eyes. "It's my fault. He trusted me. Why did I have to go on and on about my duty? There's nothing left even to bury. He vanished in the hearth just like a drop of rain."

The Snail Woman put her hand upon Shimmer's

leg and gave her a gentle shove. "I think you may have other work still to do; and he knew it."

With difficulty, Shimmer lifted her eyes from the hearth; but the dragon's shoulders sagged as if she were now burdened by a century of sorrow. "In the end, he was the bravest and best of us all." And she took up her place again at the bellows.

When Indigo and I joined her, we began to work the handle even harder than before; and the Snail Woman, with controlled waves of her fan, made the fire-rats swell even larger while her husband drove them into a frenzy.

As blasts of heat rolled over us, Indigo and I were left gasping for air; and even through her armored hide, Shimmer seemed to be feeling uncomfortable.

Standing right before the hearth must have been twice as hot. The Snail Woman had burn blisters, while the Smith had marks on his face.

Even so, they hovered by their hearth, grim and apparently as oblivious to pain as statues. And all we could do was to keep pumping away, each of us determined to do his or her part so that Thorn's sacrifice would not be in vain.

Finally, the Smith turned to his wife. Even his marvelous gown was smoking. "I think the cauldron's ready."

Nodding, the Snail Woman folded up her fan; but not before we saw the scorch streaks on the surface. Tucking the fan into her sleeve, she went to the table to pick up her hammers.

At the same time, her husband reached in with his tongs and lifted Thorn out—somehow I couldn't call it the cauldron anymore. And as Thorn rose away from the hearth, he glowed with a green light like the sun seen through a leaf. For a brief moment the Smith admired it. "We did right. Look at the light. It's the light of growth and of life."

Indigo straightened up from the bellows. "And the room," she said in a voice hushed with awe, "it's twinkling."

I turned from the bellows and saw that it was true. The gold flecks embedded in the walls were flashing like miniature stars, and the animals carved into the walls began to flash as if they were alive.

As the Smith eased Thorn over the anvil, he nodded his head solemnly. "The boy might have been young, but he was wiser than any of us: He knew it *was* his time."

"And now it's ours," the Snail Woman declared, and brought down her hammer. It rang with a clear, crystalline sound that chimed through the whole mountain.

"I think the crack's smaller already," the Smith grunted.

Shedding our robes, Shimmer, Indigo and I crowded anxiously around the anvil just out of range of the Snail Woman's hammers as she began to play a metallic tune on Thorn. "It's healing," she exulted. "With the boy's help, it's healing."

Slowly, bit by bit, the crack was disappearing under the hammer blows. In fact, it really was as if the cauldron's side were healing before our very eyes; and when it was smooth once more, I could have wept.

"It's done." The Snail Woman let her hammers dangle down as if she hardly had any strength anymore; and the Smith lifted his tongs. Both their faces and hands were blistered with burns from the fierce heat of the hearth.

And then I saw a sight I never thought I would witness in my lifetime. The dragon bowed her head humbly to each of them. "I thank you, and my people thank you. We are forever in your debt."

The Smith rubbed his ears in embarrassment and glanced at the Snail Woman. When she nodded her head, he gave a piercing whistle and then faced the dragon again. "Time enough to thank us when you finally get to use it."

Shimmer's head shot up suspiciously. "I intended to use Thorn *now*." Her paw darted out to seize him, but he was still too hot even for her armored hide; and she had to yank her paw back again.

The Smith raised his tongs threateningly like a sword. "Do that again and you'll lose that paw. You promised to pay any price if we would heal the cauldron." He clanked his tongs against Thorn's side. "Well, the price is this."

Behind us, we heard a creaking and squeaking; and when we wheeled around, we saw a dozen cranes stalk into the forge through the doorway. And large, angular shadows flickered over the air well as if there were cranes flying overhead as well. Inside the hearth the fire-rats, shrunk back to their original size, peered over the edge of the wall curiously.

Shimmer stared in disbelief and outrage at the Snail Woman and her husband. "If you'd fly me on your mountain, it would not take very long to restore the sea; and then you can use Thorn in your precious war. And I will pledge myself and my clan to fight with you."

The Snail Woman rested her hammers against her shoulders, ready to swing them if necessary. "The cauldron is too valuable a weapon to risk losing."

"I disliked deceiving you." The Smith used his

tongs to lift Thorn from the anvil. "But defeating the Nameless One is more important than your own task. I swear to you that as soon as we've won that, we will restore your sea."

Shimmer pounded her tail against the floor so hard that tools fell from the table and the walls onto the floor. "The boy gave his life so I could restore the sea. Every day that they are without a home, more dragons perish."

The Smith set Thorn down. "I'm sorry for your people. But with the Nameless One free, your people are in as much danger as the rest of the world. What good is it to have a sea if the Nameless One has exterminated all dragons?"

I was torn between what I wanted to do and what I knew my master would say. "They have a point," I said uncomfortably.

Shimmer shifted so that she could watch me as well as the Smith and his wife. "So much for an ape's oaths."

The Snail Woman tried to ease my conscience. "That oath was given before the Nameless One escaped. Now we must take the mountain back into the safety of the space between the worlds and seek the remaining two masters."

"Well, I keep my oaths." Indigo picked up a pair

of tongs and joined Shimmer. The dragon swung her head, whispering to the girl, and she nodded her head in understanding.

In the meantime, though, the Smith was trying to head off a confrontation. "The Nameless One is the enemy of all righteous people. Why are we fighting one another?" He laid his tongs down so he could spread out his arms.

Shimmer tensed—like a cat getting to spring. "You and your wife are as bad as all the others. What does it matter if a little band of dragons has to suffer?"

Licking one finger, the Smith bent over and tested Thorn's side. Apparently it was cool enough to touch now. "I would think you would want to atone for freeing the Nameless One."

"My people have suffered enough." Shimmer swung her tail hard against the hearth. As the stones tumbled in, fire-rats cascaded out onto the floor. Gleefully they began scampering and frolicking around the forge.

Presumably, Shimmer had asked Indigo to provide a distraction—which she did quite capably. With her tongs she picked up one of the fire-rats and tossed it to the Smith. "Catch."

The Smith threw himself backward, bumping into the Snail Woman; and the two of them fell against the table, overturning it with a frightful clatter. The fire rat itself landed safely enough and began scuttling about, setting fire to the papers and plans that had fallen to the floor from the table.

In the meantime Indigo was snatching up more fire-rats with her tongs and pitching them about as if she had been doing that all her life. Some of them landed on the cranes, whose machinery—or whatever was inside them—went berserk. Others kept the Smith and the Snail Woman dodging—and calling out dire threats all the while.

Since Indigo had provided the best diversion anyone could want, Shimmer threw herself on top of Thorn so that her body masked what she was doing from the Smith and the Snail Woman. But when I saw her touch the pearl that I knew was hidden in her forehead, I knew she was up to some kind of magic. Sure enough, as she bent low over Thorn, I saw her whisper a transformation spell so that a hammer took the shape of the cauldron and the cauldron took the shape of the hammer.

While she was occupied with that, I took the opportunity to expand my own staff. Bending over the dragon now, I whispered, "Leave it to a master of confusion not to be confused." And I snatched up Thorn in his disguise as a hammer.

Too late, Shimmer's paw tried to snatch it back. "Traitor."

"The Smith and the Snail Woman are being most sensible," I said, and swung my staff in an arc. Shimmer lowered her paw to protect her head; but my staff swished over her skull to smash against a crane. As mechanical crane parts rained down on her back, I tucked the hammer into my robe and winked. "But when have I ever been sensible?"

I knew what my master would have wanted me to do; but unfortunately I thought I also knew what Thorn had wanted. And in the end I couldn't disappoint that brave boy. My master would just have to understand.

Suddenly, as if she were as light as a bubble, the dragon sprang up from the floor and shook off the bits of metal. "When have any of us ever been sensible?" She laughed and picked up the fake cauldron.

"Get the cauldron," the Smith commanded the cranes as he backed away from another of his pets.

It was my turn, and I became a regular whirlwind as my staff flew now left and now right, bashing and battering more cranes.

"Indigo," Shimmer called. When the girl glanced at the dragon, Shimmer jerked a claw at her back. "Get on. We've outstayed our welcome."

"And I was having so much fun." Picking up one last fire-rat, she tossed it at the Smith and stuck out her tongue. Then, dropping the tongs, she sprang upon Shimmer's back.

When Shimmer nodded at me, I picked up on my cue. Pretending to run toward the door, I bumped into her. "Oops."

Shimmer dropped the fake cauldron to the floor with a clang. Instantly, a pair of cranes seized its sides in their beaks and began dragging it away.

The Snail Woman had kept hold of her hammers, and she started forward. "That's it. Bring the cauldron to us."

"You fool ape," Shimmer pretended to rage at me as she reached for the fake cauldron. But a half dozen snapping beaks nearly took off her paw.

It was easy for me to give a good imitation of fear. "We have to get away." And I pulled at her tail, making her wince. Perhaps she'd sprained something when she'd broken the hearth wall.

However, we hadn't reckoned on Indigo in our little farce. "I'll get it," she said, and started to slide off.

Fortunately, Shimmer managed to catch her and keep her seated on the dragon's back. "No, the little fur bag's right." She glanced at the line of cranes that now formed a wall of beaks between us and the fake cauldron. "But we'll be back."

The Smith picked up the fake cauldron. "We have more important things to tend to than to conduct a feud with you."

The cranes began to advance, but the Snail Woman sighed. "Let them go. We have what we want."

Whirling, we began running down the tunnels and through the rooms toward the exit.

"The mountain," Indigo cried out in alarm, "it's growing all shadowy again."

And it was true—the solid walls were beginning to darken and blur.

"They're returning it to the space between the worlds," I panted. "Hurry. We have to get off before that happens, or we'll be trapped."

Finally, we emerged into the room where the Snail Woman's chariot still stood. There were no sentry cranes fluttering outside. I suppose they had all been summoned inside to defend the cauldron.

Shimmer thundered past it, but I paused long enough to kick at the chariot. My foot crushed the paper-thin sides of the light chariot. Shaking off the splinters, I jogged after the dragon. "That should occupy them even more."

At the exit, I could see the Desolate Mountains far below. It was already dawn in the outside world. And the next moment Shimmer had sprung into the air with Indigo upon her back.

Wrapping an arm around my belly to cradle Thorn against me, I followed her with a skip and a hop.

CHAPTER TWENTY-SEVEN

As we fell earthward, the mountain had already become a black silhouette once again. And by the time Shimmer landed in the snow, the mountain itself had vanished and the red glow was fading from the sky—which was now morning.

Indigo slid in disgust from Shimmer's back. "We left poor Thorn back up there."

With a sigh, I let myself sink slowly down onto the cold snow. "No, we didn't."

The dragon swished her tail to test it; but nothing seemed broken. "His sacrifice won't be in vain." Shimmer held out her paw.

"What kind of trick did you two pull?" Indigo demanded, annoyed that she hadn't been a party to the secret.

"It was really more a bit of sleight of hand," I explained as I pulled the disguised Thorn from my robes and handed it to Shimmer. When the dragon started to turn so I couldn't read her lips, I had to laugh. "I finally got to see your spell."

"You think you did," Shimmer said. And she kept her back to me while she transformed Thorn back. When she faced us again, she was holding the cauldron in both her forepaws. "This has cost us the best companion anyone on an adventure could ask for. He never really complained and never gave up. And he saved my life many times. And now he's made the ultimate sacrifice."

To my astonishment Indigo bowed her head to Thorn. "I'll remember you as long as I'm alive." So their little feud was finally over—much good it did Thorn.

"You'll be honored as long as one of my people exists," Shimmer promised, but suddenly she gave a shiver.

"Are you all right?" Indigo asked solicitously.

"I . . . I thought I felt a tingle," Shimmer said uncertainly.

Curious, Indigo felt Thorn and snatched her hand back right away. "I feel it too. He must be alive in there."

I placed a paw against Thorn's hard metal side and felt something tickle my palm. "Maybe it's his soul. Maybe he's still aware and trying to contact us."

"May . . . may I carry you?" Indigo asked, and put her palm against Thorn once more. She smiled almost shyly. "I think it's all right."

Tearing strips from the bottom of her tunic, she reinforced the straps before she hung Thorn around her neck.

When Indigo had remounted, I climbed into the air. "Where to? River Glen?" That was the city Civet had flooded with the waters she had stolen from Shimmer's home.

"And from there it's on to my old home, soon to be my new home." Spreading her wings, Shimmer soared up in a shower of snowflakes.

We flew down out of the mountains, and Shimmer led us unerringly to another old caravan track. Once long lines of animals had filled the passes like a living stream. Camels, horses, musk oxen—all had carried the wealth of the world over these old stones to the Inland Sea. But now it was empty except for the weeds growing up between the cracks of the stones.

Here and there we could still make out a stony mound that marked a guard tower. In other places there were the squarish outlines of houses where villages had once stood; and the valley sides still looked like sets of giant steps where the garden terraces had once been. When Civet had stolen the sea, the trade with Shimmer's people had disappeared with its waters.

We flew over barren hills where tall forests of cedar had once grown. Once the trees had been cut down, the fertile soil had washed away, leaving only these dead, rocky slopes.

As we descended once again, we passed over mounds of slag left over from mining and refining. The folk of River Glen had transformed one of the loveliest spots in the world into a wasteland all by themselves. When Civet had seen what they had done to her lovely home, she had decided to take her revenge by flooding the city. And in a way I could understand that desire.

Ahead of us was an oval of golden light. As we drew closer, I could see the sunlight reflecting from the sea like the golden scales of a dragon.

"Home," Shimmer murmured.

I could smell the salty scent of the sea. "It's a pretty enough place."

"And soon it'll be restored." She glided in low over the hills.

It had been only a short time since Civet had first

flooded that unfortunate city; but nothing stays the same. Somehow long ropes of arrowweed, which love salt water, had sprouted along the shores of the new sea.

Here and there a forlorn tower rose above the waters, forming a refuge for flocks of ducks. And there were creatures dotting the marshes that had developed at the western edge—though we were too far away to see just what the creatures were.

But beneath the bright-blue waters were the houses of River Glen, their outlines blurring when the breeze disturbed the surface of the new sea.

Circling the shore, we passed over a rocky scrap of land that jutted out into the sea. A wooden pavilion sat rotting at its top. Before the sea had flooded the valley, this had probably been a lookout point. I indicated it with my paw. "We'll need a lot of fuel for the fire."

Shimmer nodded agreeably. "And we'll have good seats for the spectacle."

When we landed, I could see that the pavilion must have been neglected even before Civet had destroyed the city. The building's bright paint had faded long ago from the ornate carvings of dragons and other animals.

Shimmer studied the carvings dreamily. "That

style dates back to when there was still an Inland Sea."

"Then when your people are back, you ought to fix up this place again." Slipping my staff from behind my ear, I lengthened it; and then, with a half dozen well-chosen blows, I demolished the ceiling and one side.

"You may have found a new profession." Shimmer laughed easily. Now that she was almost in sight of her centuries-long goal, she was as playful as a kitten.

I laid my staff down and began to build a woodpile for the fire. "If you ever get tired of being a princess, you could become a water carrier."

Shimmer was so happy that she could ignore any insult. "I'll keep that in mind if being a princess gets boring." She knelt on her hind legs, leaning out over the sea to fill Thorn with water.

Suddenly the sea seemed to explode, and a column of water fountained above Shimmer. Her body jerked forward as if something had seized it.

"No," she said, tugging back. "Traitor! Thief!"

When the spray fell back to the surface, we could see Pomfret gripping Thorn tightly from the other side. "I knew you'd come here after finding the cauldron," he cried in triumph.

Before we could go to Shimmer's aid, the giant white dog, dripping wet, barreled out of the water nearby and knocked Indigo down. I suppose once the Boneless King had a shape, he must have been able to break the spell guarding the island; or perhaps he had simply brought a jar large enough to float his pet to freedom.

I whirled around, looking for the staff that I had carelessly put down. But a golden alligator with legs as long as a dog's loped out of the water at the same time and seized my staff between its jaws. I thought again of those creatures I had seen splashing around in the marsh; and I cursed myself for not taking a better look first.

Before I could even shout a warning, another dozen long-legged alligators sprinted from the sea and threw themselves upon me. For a moment the world was a dark nightmare of golden scales and flashing teeth. And then I was lying helpless with a kiloton of alligator on top of me.

Between their legs, I could see Shimmer and her brother still struggling down by the shore.

"It's so nice to see you, sister. It's a pity I have to say goodbye." Opening his huge jaws, Pomfret's head snaked in toward Shimmer's throat.

Shimmer managed to twist her neck just enough,

so his fangs merely grazed her hide. And then Shimmer's head darted forward, and she had her brother by the back of the neck. A quick roll and she had him pinned against the rocks, ready to break his neck.

But at that moment a huge bubble floated out of the sea. And within its iridescent sides were Horn and the Boneless King. "Let him go," the Boneless King warned, "or your friends die."

"No, kill the traitor for me," Indigo called—even though the white dog was still standing on top of her.

The Boneless King clicked his tongue. "Shame on you two. It's wicked for a brother and sister to quarrel." Horn looked worn and frightened—as if the Boneless King were still working his magical masquerade.

Horn's arms twitched up, but behind him, we could see, the Boneless King's lips moved slightly, as if he were working another spell.

It was as if a giant hand had lifted Shimmer into the air and then thrown her down on the rocks like a doll. She clawed and wrestled; but she was now helpless.

When the giant bubble touched the stones, it burst with a soft, liquid pop. And the next moment, using

Horn for more magic, the Boneless King had changed the alligators back to guardsmen.

"You're becoming quite the puppeteer," Shimmer panted defiantly.

The Boneless King gestured to Pomfret, who took Thorn to him. "Hobbies help pass the long nights and keep you out of trouble. Too bad you didn't profit from my example."

Bowing so low that his snout touched the rock, Pomfret held the cauldron up to the Boneless King.

Then he turned to Shimmer "You've lost, and we've won." And he looked up at the Boneless King as if seeking permission to kill his sister.

But the Boneless King was too busy admiring Thorn. "It really is the cauldron. And it's fixed. It's poetic justice to have it serve me now." And he fondled it lovingly, cradling it like a child until I was sick, thinking that Thorn was now in his hands. He glanced around as if counting us. "But there was a boy." Suddenly he looked down at Thorn. "I see," he said. He traced the repaired side. "So that's where he is." He nodded approvingly at Shimmer. "I underestimated you."

Ashamed, Shimmer turned to Pomfret. "This isn't the Butcher," she said desperately. "It's the Boneless King."

Pomfret simply laughed. "You must be slipping, sister. You used to lie much better than that."

The Boneless King rested Thorn against his hip. "By rights," he said to us, "you should die immediately for all the trouble you've caused. But you've brought me the means to humble my enemies easily; and for that I'm inclined to offer you a sporting chance." He rubbed his chin with his free hand. "Yes, I think we'll see how you like being imprisoned for a while." He tapped Pomfret with his foot. "Come. We have preparations to make."

As guardsmen ringed Shimmer, the Boneless King and Horn mounted Pomfret. "Come, Snowgoose," he called. As guardsmen took the place of the white dog, it leaped upon the dragon's back, fastening its teeth into the robes of the nervous little wizard.

"Don't worry," Indigo said to me, "Shimmer will find a way out of this."

I had been caught up in the battle; the enormity of our failure was just beginning to sink in. Too late I realized that the Smith and the Snail Woman had been right. Thorn was far too powerful a weapon to let fall into the hands of the Boneless King. With it he could dominate humans and dragons alike, and easily carry out his plan to waste the entire world.

"She'd better," I said. "And then we'd better get Thorn back." I could only imagine what agonies he was going through now that he was the slave of the Boneless King.

In the meantime Pomfret had risen smoothly into the air and was banking toward the Desolate Mountains. But as he and the Boneless King turned, I saw the light flash from Thorn's bronze sides. It was as if Thorn were trying to reassure us even now.

I glanced over at Shimmer to see if she had seen; and I saw her touching her forehead as if scratching; and then she looked over at us and winked. Sure that her dragon friend was up to something, Indigo twisted around and grinned at me.

And suddenly I felt myself filled with hope. Compared to what we had already done, this was only a minor setback. I remembered what Thorn had said to me, and I repeated it now for Indigo's benefit. "As long as we're alive," I promised her, "we'll find a way."